Love is
a time of enchantment:
in it all days are fair and all fields
green. Youth is blest by it,
old age made benign: the eyes of love see
roses blooming in December,
and sunshine through rain. Verily
is the time of true-love
a time of enchantment—and
Oh! how eager is woman
to be bewitched!

DEAR CAPRICE

Clifford Fortune married Caprice but his brother, Luke, knew the marriage was a mistake. He could allow himself to love Caprice blindly but that would be betraying his own brother. He found himself a wife—but the defence of marriage was no defence against the cry of his heart. Every passing year deepened his love but took Caprice further beyond his reach.

JULIET GRAY

DEAR CAPRICE

Complete and Unabridged

ULVERSCROFT
Leicester

First published in Great Britain in 1960 by
Wright & Brown Ltd.,
London

First Large Print Edition
published December 1990

British Library CIP Data

Gray, Juliet, *1933–*
    Dear Caprice.—Large print ed.—
    Ulverscroft large print series: romance
    I. Title
    823'.914

    ISBN 0-7089-2328-3

Published by
F. A. Thorpe (Publishing) Ltd.
Anstey, Leicestershire
Set by Rowland Phototypesetting Ltd.
Bury St. Edmunds, Suffolk
Printed and bound in Great Britain by
T. J. Press (Padstow) Ltd., Padstow, Cornwall

1

HE was a tall man and he cast a long shadow as he stood by the lake with the sun high overhead. He stared across the water and he looked beyond its cool dark depths, the trees which fringed it on the other side throwing their own tall shadows across the water's edge; he looked at a house which was set high in a clearing and even from this distance he could pick out the blaze of colour which was the flower gardens. The big house overlooked many miles of woodland and green pasture—the lake too was in its grounds.

Luke stood with his auburn head high, the sun glinting on the coppery, burnished gold of his hair. His deep blue eyes were darker now as he stared at the house, those trees and this lake—all his and supremely beautiful—but not what he had wanted.

The famous Fortune profile was clearly marked in this man. The renowned arrogance which accompanied the good looks typified itself in his proud bearing, the jut of his chin and the poise of his head.

He turned away from the survey of the land that was now his and he fumbled in the pocket of his tweed jacket for an old and familiar friend—his pipe. He thrust it between his teeth and clamped down on it hard as he turned his footsteps back the way he had walked. It was not alight but its very presence was comforting. He whistled briefly—a sharp, piercing whistle —and a black Labrador came running from the dense foliage and bracken nearby. He scampered up to Luke and barked excitedly, then after a few seconds of running around his feet, he ran on, Luke keeping a close eye on him while he investigated interesting scents or burrowed deep into ditches and bushes.

Well, Drake at least was satisfied with his new home. He made that very evident. But a frown creased his brow as he strode on in the wake of the dog.

What freak of mentality had led his father to bequeath Veerham to his brother Cliff together with the title and only bestow Fortune Hall on his younger son. No one knew Cliff's whereabouts: it was up to the lawyers to trace him but he had always been a nomad by nature and he could be anywhere in the world. Luke doubted if his brother even knew that their father was dead and that he was now Lord Veerham; he was sure that Cliff would have little interest in title, money or estate. But Veerham was his. As a boy he had not known the same love for the place that lived in Luke's being. While he was at the University, he had made friends with a group of Socialists and during his infrequent visits to his home he had scoffed at his father's pride in his ancestry and wealth. To Luke he had said openly that he would not welcome the title which would come to him on their father's death: that he meant to live a simple life unhampered by vast wealth and the ownership of estates; that Luke was welcome to it all.

Lord Veerham had known all these things. Yet his will had bequeathed Veerham and two thirds of his wealth to Cliff: to Luke, the younger, Fortune Hall and one third of his wealth.

Luke felt very bitter as he walked around the lake to the far side and threaded his way through the woods in the direction of what was now his home. Or would be when he had put his father's house in order and left the affairs of the estate in the care of the capable manager, Lomax. Fortune Hall had not been used very often and had been allowed to fall into a poor state of neglect: the beautiful gardens were the only sign that anyone had cared for the place and this was due to the efforts of an old man who had been born and bred on the estate and had been gardener there for the last forty years. On Luke's arrival, he had found the big and lovely rooms shrouded in dust-covers. Only the kitchen quarters where lived the elderly couple who had been employed as caretakers were habitable. Already, the place was beginning to look suitable for occupation for an army of cleaners were busy setting the place to rights. They had uncovered some old-fashioned but delightful furniture which responded well to polishing. Luke was determined to bring some of the pictures he loved from Veerham and install them at Fortune Hall. Cliff would not care. It was doubtful if he would notice their absence. It was possible that he would try to sell Veerham but

4

Luke knew that the entail did not allow him to do this.

Two brothers had surely never been so dissimilar as Clifford and Luke Fortune. Cliff had inherited his mother's waywardness and love of pleasure and travel. Luke was a man who loved his home and his ancestry as much as his father had done. He was quietly proud of the Fortune lineage which Cliff openly mocked. He was loyal to his family traditions and jealous of their beautiful possessions. Veerham was a part of him and his father had always led him to believe that one day it would be his—but his will had proved that when they were still boys, he had decided on his course of action and nothing had swerved him from it—not even Clifford's rebellion against the duties of his family and his determination to lead his own life untrammelled by wealth and title. As boys, Luke and his elder brother had little in common: as men, they were worlds apart and it spoke volumes that now Luke had no idea where Cliff was and very little interest in his movements.

Francis, Lord Veerham, had married the daughter of a man who was Master of the Hounds in his county. She had died from a hunting fall only six months after the wedding. Throwing himself into a whirl of social activity in an endeavour to forget the girl he had loved so madly, Francis met Angela Clifford who was an actress. She had set out to marry him and accomplished it within three months of their first meeting. The County had been shocked by the alliance between a Fortune and an actress. Angela had never been received graciously by his friends but they tolerated her because of Veerham's wealth and social standing. When Angela died in childbirth, they soon forgot that she ever existed and gladly welcomed Francis back to the fold. After this second bereavement, he would not risk another marriage and his two motherless sons had grown up as best as they could in a big country seat with a father who displayed little interest in either of them. Cliff had enjoyed his childhood: he sought the company of the servants and Luke often wondered if this explained his socialist tendencies or if his mother's lesser birthright had had its influence on him; he was self-sufficient and contemptuous of everything connected with family or estate.

Luke had been a lonely child who found his consolation in Veerham and its beautiful surroundings: he was proud of his forebears and his family traditions: he was inclined to arrogance and could not understand his brother's desire to be accepted by the lower classes as one of them. A lot of his arrogance had been knocked out of him at public school and, later, university but his pride in his family remained and he listened to Cliff's ranting against social snobbery and the rights of the people with something akin to dislike stirring in his breast. Cliff might say vehemently that he would rather be the son of a lowly farm-worker on the estate than the heir to Veerham and all its traditions but Luke felt that this was mostly façade. His brother did not spurn the luxuries of his home or the gaiety of his social life as the son of Lord Veerham —he did not bring any of his socialist friends to Veerham and he soon discovered that socialist talk did not impress their friends and acquaintances in the county. Luke often felt that there were two sides to his brother and he liked neither of them.

So now Cliff was Lord Veerham and

with the title came Veerham itself and an income which many another man would welcome. Luke wondered how Cliff would take the news—and despite all his brother's scorn and vehement words, he felt sure that Cliff would soon be living at Veerham and enjoying all the pomp and panoply of his new status. It was easy to reject something verbally when you knew full well that one day it would be yours without fail. Not so easy to assert sincerely that you wanted none of it when it was never likely to be in your possession.

Luke sighed. Well, Fortune Hall and its estates were his and it was up to him to do what he could with them. It was useless to be bitter about something he could not alter. The title meant nothing to him. But if only he could have had Veerham—that old and beautiful house set in rolling gardens and lawns with its miles of surrounding land: the house with its histories and memories of past Fortunes and the atmosphere which was steeped in tradition; the land with its loyal tenants and verdant soil. The old order changeth —and certainly there would be a great many changes in his life now. Veerham was over two hundred miles away and in a different county. He would leave his familiar and much-loved home and surroundings. He would see little of his many friends among the county set and the tenants whom he had known since childhood. He knew that once he left Veerham he would not cross its threshold again without invitation from Cliff—and they had drifted so far apart that he doubted if they could ever again be close friends.

He made his way across the lawns and stopped to speak to the old man whose permanently-bent back was stooped over a flower-bed in full bloom.

"Well, Roper—at least I've no complaint with the gardens. If only the house had been kept in such good order . . ."

The old man straightened up and touched his cap to his new master, scanning him with rheumy blue eyes. "We can't produce so fine a show as Veerham, sir," he said slowly, "but we do our best. As to the house, sir—well, the master wasn't very much interested in it." He pushed back his cap and scratched his thatch of white hair. "I do remember the times when the master used to spend six months of the year here, sir—but that was when the Lady Mary was alive, sir. She was as pretty a picture as ever I did see— it was here they were staying when she be thrown while out hunting and the master never came here again."

Luke listened to the recital in silence. He knew that the Lady Mary had been indeed as pretty as a picture for an oil painting of her had always hung over the fireplace in the drawing-room at Veerham. He had been told that his mother had insisted on its removal when she married Francis Veerham—but that after her death his father had replaced it and to Luke this was ample evidence that Francis Veerham had only really loved one woman in his life and that was the Lady Mary.

"That's over thirty years ago," he said as the old man finished speaking. "And my father never came here again?"

"Never the once, sir. I do remember that you and your brother—Lord Veerham as he be now, I suppose—used to come here on holidays occasionally with your cousins. Gave the place an airing, like

—but I disremember that your father ever came with you."

Luke pulled at his underlip with long, sensitive fingers. He remembered that he and Cliff had spent holidays here at Fortune Hall. It had been a children's paradise with the woods and the lake and there had been children enough to enjoy it. A whole retinue of servants and nannies and tutors had accompanied them for his father had offered the place as an ideal setting for summer holidays for the younger Fortunes. The old man's words brought back a great many long-forgotten memories. His girl cousins—Sheena, Nancy and Teresa: the boys—Cliff, himself, Jonathan and Lionel; besides these Fortunes who considered themselves the elect few in the world, friends accompanied them—schoolfriends for the main part who were thrilled with Fortune Hall if not so thrilled with the Fortunes as they were themselves. Amusement rose up in him as he thought briefly of the bumptious, conceited and arrogant crew they had been, conscious—in fact, overconscious—of their heritage and lineage and making themselves insufferable to the lesser-fortunate who spent those wonderful, full weeks with them at Fortune Hall.

How many years was it now since that last holiday? He preferred not to remember and as he turned to look up at the big house with its old timbers he felt a shaft of regret, a prick of his conscience, that he had never given this place its true value. A house had stood on these same foundations long before Veerham was built: Fortunes had been born and bred on this estate long before the land which surrounded Veerham had been bought by a wealthy ancestor; this district was steeped just as much in Fortune tradition. Yet it had never had the same appeal for him or any of the others as Veerham.

The old man studied him and then, as though he sensed his thoughts, he said stiffly: "It's a grand place for all you might think of it now, sir—maybe not so fine and elegant as Veerham but I'd rather have the Hall, sir."

Luke turned and smiled at him. The smile held real warmth. "You have more pride in the place than I have, Roper."

He pulled out an old pipe and a shabby

pouch and carefully packed the bowl as he said: "Well, sir, I've been gardener here for forty years—my dad and his dad afore him were gardeners to the Fortunes. We've always done our best for the place. Ropers, you could say, have just as much a duty to their traditions as the Fortunes, sir. It's your duty to keep the house in good order and bring life back to it: it's mine to keep the garden spruce and keep the life in it." He grinned sheepishly. "I'm letting my tongue run away with me, sir —it's not my place to be telling you your duty which you know better than I, sir."

Luke smiled again. "I'll try not to let the gardens down, Roper—and I hope I shall soon be as proud of the Hall as you seem to be."

He left the old man and walked across the lawn to the house. He paused by the stone steps which led up to the big main doors and called Drake. The dog paused in his tracks, turned his head to bark defiance, and then padded on after his own pleasurable pursuits. Luke let him be and went slowly up the steps.

He entered the house and looked about him with eyes that held new interest. He laid his hand on the carved newel-posts at the foot of the wide staircase and looked into the dim upper regions. He smiled at the thought of the boy he had once been, sliding down the wide polished balustrade and taking care to stop his progress with his feet before he slammed into the newel-posts. He remembered how Cliff had once said that when he was Lord Veerham and the owner of the Hall, he would have the newel-posts removed so that his sons could slide down to the bottom. This had been some years before he professed his lack of interest in the title and all that went with it.

He walked over to the Adam fireplace and its beauty struck him with a new force. Once he had condemned it as too ornate and Cliff had said quickly that he hoped his taste would improve with time. Well, it had.

He glanced up at the glistening chandelier which hung from the ceiling and he thought of the many balls which had been illuminated by its beauty. He thought too of the many who had danced and glided over the polished floor, rustling in silks and satins, glittering with jewels.

14

Now the old house was still and silent for the army of cleaners had packed up their mops and dusters, their scrubbing-brushes and buckets, and stolen silently away. He walked into the drawing-room and surveyed the gleaming old furniture, the thick rugs underfoot, the heavy and luxurious drapes, the famous paintings which hung on the walls. One painting was a full-length portrait of a former Fortune dressed in the elegant breeches of the eighteenth century, a sword swinging at his thigh. Luke walked over and stood under it and he looked up with his brother's voice of ten, twelve—was it fourteen—years ago ringing in his ears. Cliff had said that this man, Jeremy Fortune, had been the black sheep of the family. With a laugh he added that he resembled him more than any of the ancestors and he would probably turn out to be the same.

Now Luke studied the portrait of Jeremy Fortune. The red hair was identical to Cliff's except that he wore it in the style of the period. In an old book, Luke had learned that Jeremy refused to wear a wig but grew his own hair long and wore it in the fashionable style. The piercing blue eyes—well, they were Cliff's too, lighter than his own. The full-lipped, almost sensual mouth, the chin with its hint of weakness, the long, slender nose, the sharply-etched fine cheekbones. Yes, Cliff resembled this long-dead ancestor even to the same glint in the eyes—a mockery of accepted tenets and a determination to lead his own life. Well, Jeremy had been a rogue and a scoundrel—the black sheep of his generation—and he had been killed in a duel over a woman—not even a lady of the Court but the mistress of one of his friends, who had started life in the gutter, worked her way up to the position of actress at Old Drury, and then ended her days comfortably as the mistress of several different men. So history repeated itself in small ways—for their mother had been an actress and she had attracted Francis, Lord Veerham presumably in the same way as that eighteenth-century actress had attracted Jeremy Fortune, younger son of the Earl.

He turned away from the portrait and threw himself into one of the comfortable armchairs. How long was it since he had seen Cliff? Five—six years? Then it had been a chance meeting. He had been in the stalls at a first night in London and his attention had been attracted to a party of people who were just entering a box—and Cliff had been with them, attentive to a very beautiful girl in ice-blue satin, her hair jet black and her eyes as dark as the night. By accident, she had looked down into the stalls and their eyes had met. Hers had twinkled roguishly, then she had turned to Cliff and spoken to him. Cliff had also looked down and, catching Luke's eye, had waved a casual hand and then turned back to his companions. Later, they met in the bar and Cliff had briefly acknowledged him without introducing him to his friends. He had been well-dressed, attractive, and, it seemed, a little annoyed at the meeting with his brother. Luke, amused and indifferent, had not thought any more about Cliff during the evening but they had met again in the foyer. This time Cliff had been forced—albeit reluctantly—to introduce the lovely girl to him and she had smiled warmly and said immediately that the resemblance was so marked she had been sure there must be some relationship between the two men. Then Cliff had hustled her into their waiting taxi with a curt farewell to his brother and the brief information that he was leaving for America the following week. Now Luke could not even remember the girl's name but he distinctly remembered her striking beauty.

Cliff had inherited a certain amount of money when he reached twenty-one and had immediately installed himself in a flat in London. He had returned to Veerham once or twice during the next two years—then he had gone abroad and, apart from that one encounter, Luke had not seen him since. It caused him no pain for there had been little love lost between them even as boys and he could not forget Cliff's jibes about his love for Veerham as they grew older. He had accused him of being a true Fortune and said, with a grin, that he thought himself to be a foundling. Luke had merely replied sharply that his trouble was that he inherited too much of their mother's bad blood—and Cliff had never forgiven him for this taunt.

Luke frowned. Perhaps it had been unjust for he knew little of his mother who had died when he was still only an infant. His father seldom spoke of her and he had only picked up scant information from chance remarks made by the other members of his family and from the servants who gave her little or no respect, remembering that she came from their own class but considered herself born to the purple as soon as she became Lady Veerham.

He knew that her father had been a draper in Bradford who conveniently died shortly after she went on the stage and began to attract the attention of the society dandies. Her mother had been in service and Angela had been born six months after the wedding. She herself had been as lovely as a piece of porcelain but her temper did not match the sweetness of her mould. In the drawing-room at Veerham they still had a Sèvres vase, skilfully mended, which she had once thrown across the room at her husband when he had the temerity to annoy her. Luke often wondered if his father had regretted his hasty marriage born of infatuation and desire to own this lovely creature and believed it had been a relief to him when she died, after giving him a stillborn daughter. He could never remember his father speaking of her when he was a boy. For a long time, he had believed that the spirited, handsome girl in the portrait over the mantelpiece in the drawing-room was his mother and he was convinced that his father wished it were so.

He had no memories of his mother and he had long ago left behind the regret that he had never known her. With generations of social snobbery in his make-up, he found it easy to condemn his father for such a misalliance—and it never occurred to him that Francis, Lord Veerham, might have been seeking a happiness which was denied him.

2

IT took a long time to trace Cliff but at last it was done and Luke, who had remained at Veerham until it was possible to hand over the estate affairs to his brother, began to make arrangements for his own removal to Fortune Hall.

He did not hear from Cliff but he did not expect to do so. He rode home one day from an outlying farm and as he handed his black stallion over to a groom, he heard his name called. He glanced up and saw Cliff standing on the terrace. Surprise flooded him but very briefly and his expression revealed none of it.

He nodded to the groom and walked up the wide stone steps to the terrace. Cliff advanced towards him.

"Home is the sailor, home from the sea —and the hunter home from the hills," he said lightly as he held out his hand to Luke.

"How are you, Cliff?" His clasp was firm. He swept his glance over his brother, noting the tiny lines about the blue eyes, the deep scar which furrowed his cheek, the even deeper tint of sensuality about the mouth. He looked well, tanned and handsome: his red hair glinted in the sunlight; his well-cut suit fitted him to perfection. It was with a tiny shock of surprise that he noticed too the threads of silver at his brother's temples. Cliff was, after all, not yet thirty.

Cliff, for his part, studied his brother coolly and thought that he had not changed for all the years that had passed since they last met. He still carried himself with the eternal pride of the Fortunes. The poise of his head, the carriage of his tall frame, the cool gesture of welcome and his unruffled composure all spoke of the inborn arrogance. He was as cold and calm as ever.

"I'm fine," he replied. "Well, so the old man dealt you a nasty hand, after all, Luke? I felt sure he'd see that I didn't get any of the estates or the money even if he couldn't do anything about the title. But I never did know how his mind worked— the stupid old devil!"

There was a world of contempt in the

last words and Luke struggled with his temper. He had known a great affection and respect for his father even if he had shown little interest in his sons and little love for them.

Before Luke could reply, Cliff went on: "Come into the house, old man—I'd like you to meet my travelling companion."

The invitation was given in a lordly manner and Luke could cheerfully have punched his brother's nose. Veerham was still his home for the moment and he needed no invitation to cross its portals. But he kept his temper in check and said quietly as they entered the house together: "You've done some travelling in your time, I don't doubt."

"Lord, yes—Europe, America, Australia—I don't think there's a country I haven't seen at some time or the other." Cliff grinned and put his arm about Luke's shoulders. "I've wanderlust in my blood, old man—I never was content with home pastures like you."

They entered the lounge and now Luke was surprised. He had expected a man friend, a sunbronzed traveller like Cliff. Instead a beautiful, dark-haired woman turned from the window and gazed steadily into his eyes. He caught his breath sharply. The jet of her hair, the dark glitter of her eyes the clear beauty of her features were all so familiar. She was elegantly and expensively dressed. She held a long cigarette holder and as she smiled, suddenly, richly, blue-grey smoke wreathed from her lips and mingled with the blue-black of her hair.

"Meet the wife," Cliff announced easily and then Luke thought in passing that he had indeed inherited a common streak from their mother and he felt a shudder of distaste.

"This is your wife!" he said in surprise. "But we didn't know you were married, Cliff."

He put one long slender finger against the side of his nose. "No, I don't suppose you did. I didn't think any of you were interested in what I did with my life. Caprice, come here and kiss your brother-in-law."

She moved with a rustle of skirts and an inner grace that he remembered so well. Before he could move or speak, she took his face between cool, slim hands and brushed his lips with her mouth. Then she smiled up at him slowly before she released him. It was a seductive, a provocative smile, and the blood stirred in his veins. He was angry with himself for that swift excitement for this was, after all, his brother's wife.

"We met once—at the Croesus," she said softly, huskily, and her voice was as beautiful as the rest of her. "Do you remember, Luke?"

"Yes, I remember." He spoke awkwardly. How could he have forgotten her name—Caprice—such an unusual name and yet it suited her so admirably. He moved to the decanters. "I think this calls for a drink," he said, trying to speak with ease.

"Well, I might be the black sheep of the family," Cliff said with a laugh, "but I'm not doing so badly for myself, am I?" He put his arm about Caprice's slim waist and drew her close to him with a possessive gesture. "I hope you've noticed that I'm in line with one of the family traditions— I've married a beauty."

Luke turned and studied the pair, standing so close together, and once again he felt a shudder of distaste. She was beautiful and it disturbed him that she should be wasted on his shallow, dissolute brother.

He did not reply to this sally. He handed them both a wine-glass which contained an exquisite sherry whose amber depths reflected the light. He raised his own glass. "Success and happiness, Cliff. Welcome to the family and may you know every happiness, Lady Veerham." He smiled and drained his glass.

Cliff laughed. "Trust Luke to play the pompous ass. I'm surprised you didn't congratulate me on my new title—but I suppose that would be asking too much of you, noble as you are. I bet you've hoped against hope that I'd get myself killed wandering in foreign parts, old man."

Caprice said gently, "Please, Cliff—that isn't in very good taste."

Another surprise for Cliff took the rebuke very well. He bestowed a light kiss on his wife's hair and said, "Sorry, darling. Erase it from the minutes, Luke —and no hard feelings, eh?"

Luke's eyes had glinted like steel but now he relaxed and said smoothly, "You'll find that everything is in order, Cliff. Lomax manages the estate very well—he's extremely efficient and if you keep him on, you'll have no worries. The lawyers told you that Fortune Hall is mine?"

"Yes. You aren't going to live in that derelict old barn?"

"I am indeed. It isn't so derelict as you think. I hope you and Caprice will honour me with a visit before long then you may see for yourself that it's quite as lovely as Veerham."

Cliff chuckled and looked down at Caprice. "It might be amusing to honour Luke with a visit, mightn't it?" His tone was mocking and Luke regretted his pedantic choice of words. "We used to spend our holidays there as kids—Luke fished me out of the lake once and saved my life—I've often wondered why. It's rather a pleasant old place—but falling to pieces."

"Only through neglect," Luke put in. "I've already made great changes and in time it will be as much a showpiece as Veerham."

"But Veerham will always have the

advantage while it has Caprice to add to its attractions," Cliff said lightly.

Caprice moved away from his restraining hand. "You must forgive Cliff." She addressed Luke. "I'm afraid he acts rather like a collector with a rare and valuable possession where I'm concerned. I'm always reminding him that beauty is in the eye of the beholder."

"Luke would have to be blind not to acknowledge your beauty, my lovely one," Cliff said quickly. "And you are a rare and valuable possesion. I married you for your looks—I thought you knew that."

Luke, watching carefully, noticed a slight shadow across the woman's lovely face and he wondered. It was gone in a moment and then she bantered lightly: "I thought my money was my main attraction."

"Let's say it was an added incentive." Cliff drained his glass. "This is excellent sherry. I'll have another, Luke. I see that most of the servants are the same—the old order apparently never changeth at Veerham!"

"It will soon," Luke retorted, refilling

his brother's glass. There was a grim note in his reply.

Caprice caught his eyes and smiled. "You'll be sorry to leave here?" she questioned gently. "I'm feeling guilty about turning you out of your home."

"Fortune Hall is my home," he said quietly, but firmly. "This is the home of Lord Veerham—and he is standing beside you."

Lunch was a difficult meal. Cliff was in high humour and because his humour had always contained a slightly malicious streak, many of his remarks held a faint jibe. With an effort, Luke gritted his teeth and managed to return pleasant and non-committal replies. Caprice toyed with her food and made little contribution to the conversation except when Cliff spoke directly to her. Occasionally, she looked up from her plate and met Luke's eyes and he read an appeal in their depths as though she sensed the barbs behind her husband's apparently light remarks and apologised for him. Luke endeavoured to reassure her with a fleeting smile, a warmth in his eyes, a gesture of his hand. Cliff's words had the power to annoy but not to hurt.

After the meal, Cliff announced that he was going to look over the stables and see if the horseflesh was good enough for the new Lord Veerham. He swung from the drawing-room, leaving Caprice and Luke alone. She took a cigarette from a slim gold case and he moved quickly to flick a lighter into flame for her. Then she smiled and offered the case to him.

"No, thanks. If I may, I'll smoke my pipe."

"Please do. Men who smoke pipes are usually so masculine," she said quietly. Her eyes appraised him coolly and he found himself puzzled by her. He could not assess her true value. He was not sure if her eyes glittered with wicked innocence or innocent wickedness—and there was a world of difference between the two.

He sat down opposite her and kindled his pipe. She watched him, laying back in the deep chair, perfectly composed, her eyes half-smiling and her lips curved a mere fraction. He looked up and met her gaze and once again felt that brief, disturbing stirring of his blood. She was more beautiful than he had remembered —and the memory of her had been vivid enough. Following the train of his thoughts, he said abruptly: "It must be five or six years since we met at the Croesus—yet you remembered instantly."

She smiled now, a full generous smile that showed white even teeth and the tip of a tiny pink tongue. His heart began to pound. "I have a long memory," she said slowly, huskily.

"Have you been married long?" he asked quickly to cover his rising emotions.

"Long?" She repeated his question and there was a strange note in her voice. "An eternity," she said quietly. "Two years," she added on a firmer note.

He smiled. "And it seems an eternity?" He did not wait for her reply. "Cliff is a strange devil—why didn't he write to us? My father would have been pleased to know the woman who would one day be Lady Veerham."

She shrugged, a mere movement of her slim, lovely shoulders. "Cliff pleases no man but himself. But you surely know that better than I do."

Carefully, he re-kindled his pipe which had died. "Cliff and I have never been very close. I should imagine that you know more of him than I do."

"I hope you like him more than I do," she said, and again that strange note in her voice.

He looked at her quickly, startled. "But you're his wife. Surely you love him."

"Love—passion—oh yes, that. But I was talking of liking. One can love a man without liking the man he is," she said.

He did not like the turn the conversation had taken. He said abruptly: "What do you think of Veerham? Do you think you'll be happy here?"

She smiled enigmatically. "You have one of Cliff's traits, anyway. He always changes the subject when he doesn't like what I say. Veerham?" Again that fleeting shrug. "I don't suppose we'll spend much time here. Cliff was born with the wanderlust—we'll be abroad again before long, I expect."

He felt a stirring of bitterness. "Yes, Cliff was never content with home pastures."

Her eyes held something of sympathy. "I'm sorry, Luke," she said, surprisingly. "It must be rather hard to be the youngest son and know that Cliff doesn't give a damn for his heritage."

He was disturbed by her perspicacity then he reminded himself that Cliff would naturally have impressed upon her, with much scorn, that his brother worshipped every acre of Veerham and resented the fact that he would not inherit it on his father's death.

"That's one of the twists of Fate," he said lightly. "But I have Fortune Hall and I shall be quite content with my lot. You will come and see it, I hope?"

She nodded. "I'll persuade Cliff to bring me. It won't be very difficult." Noting the firmness of her small chin he felt sure that she knew how to handle her husband and he knew a momentary pleasure that he would be able to show this strangely beautiful woman all over his own house and land. She went on slowly: "How wise you are to accept things and make the best of them. That is one thing that Cliff cannot do—he is always railing at one thing or another when it doesn't turn out the way he wishes. As for me, I learnt the lesson of acceptance long ago. It does no good to rebel."

Luke longed to know more about this woman. A hundred questions burned in his brain but he did not speak them. He rose to his feet. "Has Cliff shown you over the house yet?"

"No. Would you?" She rose too with a swift, graceful movement. "It's very old, isn't it?"

"It was built in 1735 on the foundations of a much older building. There have been several improvements throughout the years, though—every Fortune—or, I should say, every Lord Veerham—makes some additional improvement. My father had electricity installed, for instance, and put in an extra bathroom."

He preceded her from the room and he showed her the two big reception rooms, the oak-panelled dining-room, the massive, high-ceilinged hall with its marble floor of different coloured squares, the ancient carved staircase, the picture gallery, the musicians gallery, the eight bedrooms. When they returned to the hall again, he indicated a green baize door with the information that it led to the staff quarters. "My grandfather built an annexe which he called the guest house—I expect you saw it across the lawns. He used to entertain very much and very lavishly but my father withdrew a great deal from society after my mother's death and the place hasn't seen much activity since then. You can see the red roofs of the stables in the distance and, just beyond that, the home farm."

She laid a hand on his arm. "It's quite a heritage," she said. "I hope Cliff and I can live up to it."

"Oh, Cliff's a Fortune—he'll live up to it." He told her of the portrait which hung at Fortune Hall and of Cliff's likeness to Jeremy Fortune. He did not tell her the story of Jeremy's unfortunate end.

"Cliff may be a Fortune," she said when he had finished, "but he has a strong streak of Clifford in him too." There was a slight sneer in her voice.

He looked down at her. "Cliff's mother was also my mother," he reminded her.

"I know that—but you've inherited far more of the Fortune characteristics than Cliff."

He laughed slightly. "You hardly know me, my dear Caprice—how can you possibly be so sure of that?"

She took her hand from his arm and walked into the drawing-room. "I know Cliff—and you two are as different as chalk and cheese."

Cliff came into the room at that moment, whistling blithely. He was very much Lord of the Manor in his attitude as he entered and he announced immediately: "The old man didn't have much knowledge of horseflesh in recent days, did he? I shall have to make some drastic changes. The only decent stallion is that big black one—what's its name—Royal?"

"He's my horse," Luke said quietly. "He's the finest mount in the district."

Cliff grinned. "I commend your taste, Luke. I suppose I can't prevent you from taking the best animal in the stables with you? Will you sell him?"

"No, I'm afraid you can't prevent me—and I've no intention of selling Royal," Luke said firmly.

"I'll soon replace him," Cliff said firmly and confidentialy. He ran his hand lightly over Caprice's raven hair. "Well, what do you think of my stuffed shirt of a brother, sweetheart? I gather you've been getting to know each other while I've been gone. I hope he hasn't filled you up with a pack of nonsense about me."

Luke said stiffly, "I've been showing Caprice over the house."

Cliff grimaced. "Dull old mausoleum, isn't it, darling? We'll have to liven it up a bit if we're going to live here for any length of time." He glanced at his watch. "We must be leaving," he said swiftly.

"You're not staying?" Luke asked in sudden dismay.

"No. We're dining with friends tonight. You'd better tell the servants to expect us at the weekend. I suppose you'll be leaving before then, Luke?" It was more of a command than a supposition.

Luke paled slightly but he nodded. "Yes. I shall leave on Friday—the place will be entirely in your hands then. I hope you are fully aware of your duty to Veerham."

"Don't talk piffle, dear brother. The days of duty are long dead. I'll go and get the car, Caprice—you powder your nose or something." He clapped Luke on the shoulder. "Maybe we'll run down to Fortune Hall and look in on you one day, Luke—I'd like to see the old place again.

We had some good times there in our youth."

He was gone in a moment. Luke thought in passing that Cliff had always shown this restlessness, this need for moving on and away from Veerham. His heart was sad within him as he remembered that soon, very soon, he too would be moving on and away from Veerham.

He was startled when Caprice came close to him and once again cupped his face within her two hands. "Dear Luke," she murmured. "I will look after Veerham for you."

He gazed deep into her eyes. "I believe you will," he said slowly.

She smiled up at him and he was filled with the longing to draw her close, into his arms, against his heart. "Don't forget all about me," she whispered huskily, then she pressed her cool mouth against his for a long moment. When she drew away, a long sigh escaped her. "How I wish Cliff was more like you," she said longingly then she dropped her hands and turned away. She walked from the room without a backward glance.

Cliff tooted his horn impatiently and

Luke moved to the windows. He watched the car surge swiftly down the drive with the impatience of its driver and then it turned through the big wrought-iron gates and was lost to sight.

Luke stood at the window for a long time. The impression of her mouth lingered on his lips. The coolness of her hands seemed still about his face. In his nostrils was still the faint breath of perfume which permeated from her when she stood so close to him.

She was a strange woman—a beautiful woman and, he sensed, an unhappy one. Yet she had said she loved Cliff and there was about his casual manner towards her an indication that he loved her in his shallow fashion.

He shook his head and stirred impatiently. Why the devil should his mind be possessed with thoughts of Caprice? He had seen her only twice—the first time in a brief encounter—and now as his brother's wife. She was a bewitching and provocative woman who had the power to disturb a man's blood and she knew it full well. She had been gifted with fascination, with a seductively husky voice, with beauty and lithe grace, with a sensuous body and glittering eyes which drew and held a man's gaze—and she knew all these things and delighted in her power and used all its force on any man who attracted her briefly.

He dismissed her from his thoughts with the last rider that she suited Cliff for she herself was shallow and flirtatious—had she not kissed him with lingering passion and the promise of fuller delights as soon as her husband's back was turned and glorying in the knowledge that she stirred his blood and quickened his heartbeats.

He was angry with himself for taking her seriously, even for a moment, and he determined that once he was at Fortune Hall he would forget her completely despite the last plea she had made to him.

3

HE knew that his new home could never fill the aching void in his heart which was his longing for Veerham—yet he was content, as he had told Caprice that he would be. He felt a strange thrill of pride whenever he entered the lovely old house, or crossed the beautifully-kept and verdant lawns, or returned the greeting of one of his tenants as he walked or rode about the district. He had never owned Veerham—but Fortune Hall and Mallingham was his and he knew pride of possession.

At first, the tenants looked askance at this new squire and their greetings, while respectful, lacked warmth. But he gradually won over the cautious country people with his swift smile, the easy manner, his obvious knowledge of country affairs and his way with animals.

Soon he was spoken of proudly as "the master" and they spoke among themselves of his family name and his heritage.

The house itself seemed to welcome his presence and responded to the new life within it. A peaceful atmosphere pervaded the big rooms and Luke felt that he had never been so quietly happy in his life. He had known happiness at Veerham but always there had been the thread of bitterness, of vain hopes: the knowledge that Veerham could never be his; the vague perception that the alien blood in his veins separated him a little from the many Fortunes who lined the picture gallery and that his father would never forgive himself for marrying Angela Clifford and begetting two sons who had the same blood as a draper, a housemaid and an actress mingling with the ancient blood of the Fortunes and the other excellent families that the Fortunes had married into.

He soon became well known in the district: not only to the tenants but also to his neighbours who called themselves the "county". They too were wary of him at first, despite his old and respected name, but soon they accepted him and sent him invitations for this or that social gathering. He was a keen huntsman and a good rider: his stallion was much admired and they marked him up as a man who knew his horseflesh; he was handsome and charming and eligible, and the parents of unmarried daughters welcomed him warmly into their midst. The daughters themselves found him attractive but aloof and his inborn arrogance rebuffed them a little.

The days and then the months passed swiftly. He watched the changing seasons and loved Fortune Hall more with every change. He took a great interest in the home farm and in the stables, in the upkeep of the grounds. He fenced off a dangerous part of the lake and then let it be widely known that he would gladly permit anyone to use its cool waters for pleasure. The woods too were no longer guarded jealously and he felt a warmth steal over him whenever he strolled about his land and heard the shrill cries of children who played in the woods or swam in the lake.

It was two years since he had left Veerham and now he could think of his old home without the familiar pang of longing and the shaft of bitterness. He had seen Cliff only the once in all that time when he was staying with friends fifteen miles away and he drove over to Fortune Hall. He had not seen Caprice at all. Cliff had explained that his wife was staying with her family in Cornwall and that he was on the loose for a few weeks. He had added this last with a grin and a wink for his brother which implied that he meant to make the most of his freedom. It had been relief which flooded Luke as his brother finally left the house. Cliff was looking older than his thirty-two years and his body was beginning to assimilate a little weight. Luke had felt that he did not want Cliff's presence to taint the atmosphere and, as usual, it had been difficult to restrain his tongue from giving Cliff sharp retorts to his jibes and innuendoes.

He was riding home one afternoon from the hunt, resplendent in his pink coat, a hunting crop in his hand, when the sound of a fast car behind him in the lane made him pull Royal sharply over to the hedge. They were ambling along slowly and he was enjoying the scents and sweetness of the Spring afternoon, the quiet peace which pervaded the countryside. Suddenly all was disrupted with the swish of tyres and the roaring of engine as the car shot past him. Royal reared and fretted while Luke kept a firm hand on the reins and muttered a brief curse after the distant car.

He reached the stables and attended to Royal himself. He was a little anxious about the stallion's fetlock for he had limped slightly on the way home. It was some time before he finally went up to the house and he was met by his butler with the news that Lady Veerham was waiting for him in the drawing-room.

He stared at the man in disbelief. "You must have the name wrong, Vernon," he said sharply.

"No, he hasn't," a soft voice said behind him and he spun on his heel to face a smiling Caprice. "I thought you were never coming, Luke—I passed you ages ago."

He walked past her into the drawing-room, pulling off his gloves. "You were driving that car?"

"Yes."

"Too fast," he said curtly.

She stood in the doorway watching him, that too familiar smile curving her lips and her eyes were laughing mocking him. "It's two years since I saw you, Luke—and you don't seem at all pleased that I've kept my promise."

"Promise?" He frowned.

"You've forgotten," she said gently. "Well, it's a long time ago now. I've come to see Fortune Hall—and what I've seen so far I think delightful."

"Where's Cliff?"

She pouted and then laughed lightly. "Cliff? Oh, he's abroad—alone, I believe, but one can never tell with Cliff."

He said abruptly: "You'll forgive me, Caprice. I must change."

"Of course. I'll explore the gardens while you're gone—if I may?"

He felt that she was laughing at him again. "Please—go where you like, Caprice." He walked to the door and she stood aside to let him pass. She caught his arm and he paused, surprised. With a light, easy movement, she touched her fingers first to her own lips then pressed them against his. It was an endearing gesture and a relief, for he had been afraid that she meant to kiss him full on the mouth.

"Dear Luke," she said quietly. Then she smiled. "I can do better than that—

46

but not with servants hovering in the background." She patted his arm. "Go and change, my dear."

When he came down, she was not in the drawing-room. He poured himself a drink, drained it quickly. Why had she come to Fortune Hall? Not simply to see the place —he wasn't that naïve. Then to see him —but why? Two years had passed and neither had given the other a thought. He pulled himself up sharply. That wasn't strictly true but he had chased away the fleeting thoughts that came unbidden to his mind and gradually they had come at longer intervals. He wondered what had been behind her remark about Cliff—was he unfaithful to her and did she know it? She seemed singularly unconcerned. Perhaps she was frequently disloyal to Cliff—he would not doubt it, he thought grimly, remembering the way she had kissed him two years ago and the invitation in her very attitude.

"I know what you're thinking," she said softly. He did not turn round. He was startled because he had not heard her enter the room. Calmly, apparently unruffled, he poured another drink.

"Would you like a drink?" he asked quietly.

"Do you have some of that delightful sherry?" she asked.

Without a word, he poured some from a decanter into a glass and turned to hand it to her.

"What was I thinking?" he asked lightly.

"You were wondering why I came—and I'm sure you think I had an ulterior motive."

He sat down in a deep armchair and studied the contents of his glass. "You're very perceptive."

"Not at all. You're Cliff's brother—and there are times when he has a very evil turn of mind. I'm disappointed to find the same in you." But her voice was light and mocking and scarcely did he think she meant her remark seriously.

"Do you really expect me to believe that you've driven from Veerham simply to look over my home?"

"Cliff's away and I'm lonely. I suddenly remembered that I have a most charming brother-in-law and I decided to pay him a visit. I've already told your housekeeper to prepare a room for me, Luke—was I too presumptuous?"

"Then you intend to stay?"

"For a few days. I've come to brighten your solitary existence." She smiled at him and he noticed that her small pink tongue darted across her lips. He felt that old prickling of excitement within him. "Why haven't you married, Luke?" she asked abruptly. "There must be plenty of women who would be willing to marry you." She put her wine-glass down on the table by her side with a sharp little sound and took her cigarette case from her handbag.

"I daresay there are, but I've yet to find the woman that I'd be willing to marry," he said and he smiled.

"It seems so topsy-turvy," she said. "Cliff is the one who should never have married—he likes his freedom too much —and you, who are so essentially the family man, remain a bachelor."

"I doubt very much if Cliff regrets his marriage," he said calmly.

"I didn't say that he regretted it—I merely said that he likes his freedom and that's the truth. Now he's going to be a family man whether he likes it or not. I'm going to have a child, Luke." She said the words flatly and without emotion, without any of the joyous anticipation that one would expect with such a statement.

He stared at her. Then, with an effort, he collected his thoughts and said, "Does one offer congratulations? It's about time, isn't it? You've been married about four years and Cliff should ensure the entail."

"I don't think it's a matter for congratulation," she said wearily.

He smiled at that. "Oh, come! You're not asking me to believe that you aren't very pleased with yourself? Every woman thinks it an achievement to present her husband with an infant."

"Not this woman."

He looked anxious. There was sincerity in the abrupt words. "You really mean that you don't want children, Caprice?"

"Not Cliff's." Then she smiled at the look of astonishment which crossed his face. "My dear Luke, don't look so horrified. I'm a great believer in the truth. You may as well know too that I'm no longer in love with Cliff—I doubt now if I ever loved him."

"What are you going to do?"

"Do? Have the child, of course. What do you expect, Luke? I married Clifford, Lord Veerham, for better or worse—it's no one's fault but my own if it's turned out for the worse." Scorn and mockery mingled in her tone. "I know my duty," she went on. "Which is to provide an heir for the title—which is the only reason why Cliff gave me this child. Don't imagine for one moment that Cliff loves me any more than I love him. Marriage was a necessary evil to him—I was both wealthy and beautiful and on the spot. I was also young and healthy and it was a fairly safe bet that I'd produce an heir in time. Time? As you pointed out, we've been married four years. Still, what do you expect—I see very little of Cliff, you know. If he's not abroad, he's in London—and if I'm in London too, then he's busily entertaining friends and being entertained in turn. I'm a neglected wife, Luke—didn't you know?"

He rose and went to her, taking her hands. "My dear, you're tired and over-wrought. I shall forget all you've said

51

because I don't think you mean a word of it."

She looked up into his face. "Dear Luke," she said. "Burying your head in the sand again. I know so little about you —and yet I know everything there is to know. Does that sound strange?"

Luke looked into those dark, glittering eyes and he thought of the news she had brought. So she was to bear Cliff's child —another one to bear the Fortune name. He ignored the stirring of pain in his heart and knew only the touch of her cool hands, the gaze of her beautiful eyes.

"I believe you do," he said slowly. "Caprice, why won't you be happy? I know you're not—you've never been happy with Cliff—yet you once told me that you loved him and I won't believe that love dies that easily."

She laughed huskily and there was real merriment in the sound. "Why won't I be happy?—because I'm a rebel, Luke. I always have been. I want the thing that's always out of reach—and I don't want the thing that's close at hand." She rose to her feet, releasing her hands from his firm, reassuring clasp. "Will you forgive me if I go to bed, Luke? It was a long drive and I am tired."

"Of course," he said swiftly. "I'll arrange for dinner to be sent up to you."

"Tomorrow I shall be in better humour," she promised lightly, "and I'll try not to disturb you with the truth." She went towards the door, then she paused and looked back, and he noticed that her eyes were glistening now with unshed tears. He took a step towards her and she said quickly, "Luke, you don't mind that I came to you?"

He shook his head. "No, Caprice."

There was a trace of the old mockery in the way she tilted her head and smiled. "I have doubts about your honesty—but never mind. Will you kiss me, Luke?" There was invitation in her eyes.

Luke stood looking at her for a long moment and perhaps his expression reflected the feeling of dismay, the momentary contempt.

The smile lingered richly on her lips and now it reflected in her dark eyes. Then she laughed at him. "Luke, you just don't know what to make of me, do you?" Her voice was slow and husky. "A woman should be always a mystery to men." Then she left the room and silently closed the door behind her.

Luke stood with clenched hands then abruptly he turned to the window, fumbling for his pipe. He put it between his teeth and bit hard on the stem. He stared without seeing across the beautiful countryside and for once the familiar pleasure in his surroundings did not sweep over him.

He was filled with both a violent longing and at the same time a bitter contempt for his desire. What right had he to desire Caprice merely because she offered a provocative invitation? She was his brother's wife and he determined to drive out the dishonourable thoughts, to crush down the excitement she caused with her dark, glowing beauty, the rich, sensual smile and the seductively husky voice. She disturbed and bewildered him. She was right—he did not know what to think of her.

Was the wicked gleam of her eyes deliberate and calculated? Or was she totally unaware of the effect she could have on a man's emotions? Did she set out to attract and excite—or did he read meanings into what were really innocent and affectionate gestures? Was she wholly bad—or were the unexpected tendernesses a revelation of the real woman and the rest merely a façade?

He had no answers for his questions. He knew that he must not allow his thoughts to dwell on her—that way lay danger. She was Cliff's wife and within her she carried Cliff's child—the future Lord Veerham possibly. He told himself firmly that he must discount the things she had said with bitterness behind them. In her condition, a woman tended to exaggerate matters and it would be very wrong of him to assume that she was indeed unhappy with Cliff or that their marriage was a failure.

He dined alone that evening but he was very conscious of the woman in her room above. Vernon came in and bent down to say: "Lady Veerham wishes you to join her for coffee in her room, sir."

It was on the tip of his tongue to say: "Tell her to go to blazes!" but instead he pushed aside his napkin and rose to his feet. "Very well, Vernon. Serve coffee in Lady Veerham's room." He walked slowly up the wide staircase, his hand running lightly on the polished balustrade. Why this imperious command? With an effort, he adopted a cool and indifferent pose and knocked lightly on the door of her room.

"Come in, Luke," she called softly and as he opened the door he felt a slight annoyance that she was so confident of his obedience to her command.

She was not in bed. A flimsy scarlet negligee barely covered the even flimsier black nightdress and the creamy white column of her throat rose up from the folds of chiffon. She was lounging on a comfortable divan and he noticed that the small, slender feet were bare.

She smiled up at him. "Sit down, Luke," she invited. "I've just enjoyed an excellent meal—your cook is to be congratulated. But it was very lonely—and I couldn't stand the solitude any longer." Her eyes darkened suddenly. "I hate being alone," she said vehemently.

Luke sat down in the armchair she indicated. He was tense and edgy. "Shouldn't you put on something a little warmer," he said and knew that his voice rasped harshly. "These Spring evenings can be very cool."

She looked at him intently. At last she said, "I believe you're a prude, Luke—it's surprising that two brothers should be so different in character."

He knew that he flushed for the blood was hot in his face for a moment. "I'm not a prude," he said stiffly. "I'm merely concerned with causing gossip among the staff. I would prefer you to wear something a little less revealing."

Caprice laughed. "The servants. Let them talk—I'm not worried."

"Perhaps you think that Lady Veerham —like Caesar's wife—is beyond reproach —that, in fact, you may do as you please without fear of condemnation?"

She was pleating the folds of her negligee with restless fingers and suddenly he longed to lay his hand on hers to calm the nervous movements. She seemed at her ease yet her hands betrayed her.

"I don't take the title that seriously," she replied smoothly.

"Where did you meet Cliff?" he asked abruptly.

She wrinkled her nose prettily. "Must

57

we talk about Cliff? Very well—if you prefer safe ground. We met at a cocktail party—mutual friends. It's a long time ago now—I was seventeen. I found him amusing and attractive."

"Seventeen!" he exclaimed. She had seemed so mature that night at the theatre.

She was percipient. She said lightly: "You're thinking of our first meeting at the Croesus, Luke. That was a few years later. Cliff and I had been around together. He told me of his plans to sail across to France in his yacht and from there around the coast to Italy. I did a lot of sailing when I was a child—it sounded fun and I agreed to join him." She shrugged briefly. "It was fun—Cliff can be a wonderful companion when he chooses."

"The sea has never attracted me," Luke said.

Coffee arrived at that moment, brought by an imperturbable Vernon. He placed the tray on a small table which he moved closer to Caprice and then silently left the room. Luke watched as she deftly poured the fragrant hot liquid. Her movements were neat and capable and, as ever, graceful.

She handed Luke his coffee and then thoughtfully began to stir her own. "Cliff loves the sea—he told me that one of your ancestors was a sailor and that he had inherited something from the Fortunes."

Luke frowned briefly. "Knowing Cliff, he was referring to Garth Fortune who was a brigand and a pirate with a little bit of smuggling as a sideline. He died at sea after an engagement with some French rivals."

"We met you soon after we had returned from Paris. We spent six months there on the Left Bank; before that we lived in Monte Carlo for a year. The week after the theatre visit we left for America. We went on to Australia from there . . ."

"You were married by then?"

She laughed lightly. "No. It didn't seem to matter. Cliff cares nothing for conventions—don't you know that?—and I was madly infatuated. When we were in Australia, another man began to pay his attentions to me and Cliff was furious. He half killed the poor devil one night—the next morning he and I were married in Perth."

Her words were confirming the dreadful doubt in his mind. She had lived with Cliff for years before she married him and like Cliff, she cared nothing for convention. She was a bewitching, disturbing and immoral woman who, having tired of her husband, was now seeking distraction elsewhere. His expression was grim and he felt sick with disappointment.

She waited until he was compelled to look at her. Then she smiled slowly, that rich disturbing smile, which showed her lovely teeth and the tip of her tongue. But there was more than invitation in the smile —there was amusement too.

"Dear Luke," she said with that odd inflection which always caused a tremor to run through his body. "I've shocked you. What does it matter that I was Cliff's mistress for seven years before I married him?—eventually I married him." She laughed. "He made an honest woman of me—in his own words." Her face clouded briefly. "I regret to tell you, Luke, that there is an essentially common streak in your brother. Before I married him, I found it attractive—now it revolts me."

"Why did you marry him?" he asked stiffly.

She replaced her cup with a sharp little

60

sound. "I've been wondering that for a long time. Because I thought I loved him, I suppose—but it was the kind of love that flourished while we flouted convention—and died a sudden death when I became his wife and found that he treated me like a husband instead of a lover." Her lip curled with contempt. "Now he finds me a bore—and he travels abroad without me —probably in the company of a new mistress." Her voice was cold and bitter.

Luke rose and put his cup on the tray. He found that he was trembling. "Why are you telling me all this?" he demanded.

She put out a hand and caught his fingers. She stroked the long, sensitive fingers gently. "Because you wanted to talk about Cliff—and because I don't want you to have any illusions about me, Luke." Suddenly she released his hand and slipped her arm about his neck, drawing him down to her, raising her slim and beautiful body to reach him. Before he could move or protest, her mouth was on his—warm and hungry and moist, eager and ardent.

He fought down the rising tide of desire and with pounding heart he firmly released himself from her embrace and straightened up. She was smiling triumphantly and he knew swift anger. Harsh words were on his lips yet he found it impossible to speak them. He strode from the room and slammed the door sharply. There were names for a woman like Caprice—yet he rejected each and every one of them as they flashed into his mind. He would not believe evil of her—behind that triumphant smile was a gleam of mockery and he was convinced that if he had tried to take matters any further she would have rebuffed him coolly and capably. There were women like that—and Caprice was surely one of them. It thrilled her to know her own power over men—but nothing would surely persuade her to be unfaithful to her husband and the father of her child.

It had been difficult to quench the flame of desire but he knew that he would have been filled with utter and complete self-loathing if he had taken the favours which his brother's wife had blatantly offered.

4

HE did not see Caprice at breakfast. After the meal, he walked down to the lake with Drake running on ahead, uttering a joyous exclamation every so often at the wonders of nature.

His thoughts were of Caprice this morning. So had his dreams been— violent, disturbing dreams which caused him to move restlessly in his bed.

He thrust his hands deep into his jacket pockets and strolled aimlessly, the sun warm on his bare head, bracken snapping underfoot.

He felt like a drowning man who tried desperately to keep his head above water. Caprice had bewitched him. He no longer denied this. But he knew that for the sake of his peace of mind, he must ignore this upheaval of his emotions and continue as best he could to retain the even tenor of his life.

Now he admitted that he had not forgotten her all those years after their first meeting in London. It had been a brief encounter but her beauty and vitality had left its impression and he must often have thought of her, albeit subconsciously, in the years that followed. Then Cliff had introduced her casually as his wife—and his heart had leaped wildly as she turned to regard him coolly. The touch of her lips, cool and light though it was, had seared his emotions.

That had been two years ago and no woman had attracted him in all that time because he was unconsciously seeking a woman like Caprice—and there was only one Caprice. He remembered his disappointment when Cliff had arrived unexpectedly at Fortune Hall—alone. He had not thought of it as disappointment at the time. Only now was he coolly analysing his emotions and going back over the past with that knowledge in his heart that he was in love with his brother's wife.

He stopped dead in his tracks as the words echoed in his brain—in love with his brother's wife. It was the first time he had formulated his emotions so definitely.

He walked on, dispirited and confused, his mind in turmoil. What could he do but try to forget Caprice; to impress upon himself that she could never be his no matter how much he wanted her.

Why had she disillusioned him the night before? What was her motive? Was she aware that he loved her, in that strange perceptive way woman have of knowing these things, and had tried in a small way to impress upon him how worthless and immoral she was as a person?

He stood by the lakeside and ran his fingers wildly through his red-gold hair until it stood rampant. The water was cool and deep and peaceful, the sunlight shimmering on its surface. Suddenly Luke was disturbed by the water. This apparently pleasant lake was like Caprice—lovely to look at, cool and inviting on the surface— and beneath? Hidden, ugly depths: treacherous snares; dangerous secrets. One could wade into the lake's welcoming embrace and walk blindly out, going deeper all the time without thought for results, and then at last one could drown in its depths, be caught up for ever in that embrace, and never know life or sanity again. So could he snatch at the invitation of Caprice's embrace. He could allow himself to love her blindly and deeply without thought for the ending—and then at last one would be beyond salvation, betraying one's own brother and one's own honour, never knowing peace of mind, which was sanity, or happiness, which was life, in the future.

He stooped and picked up a round, smooth stone. He skimmed it across the surface of the lake and it broke into ever-widening ripples, destroying the calm and the glitter and the beauty. So one could pierce Caprice's cool sophistication and self-possession and know the agitation behind the calm, the dullness behind the glitter, the canker behind the beauty.

He allowed these and like thoughts to invade his mind and knew that he was deliberately trying to destroy the love within him for Caprice.

When he returned to the house, he asked Vernon if Lady Veerham had come down yet. The butler handed his master a salver on which lay a sealed envelope. "Lady Veerham left in her car half an hour ago, sir. She left this message for you."

With trembling hands and a sickness in the pit of his stomach, Luke took the envelope and stared down at it. It was inscribed in a sprawling yet attractive hand simply with his name. He turned and entered the drawing-room and closed the door firmly behind him. Caprice had gone. He knew that without breaking the seal of the envelope. She had waited until he left the house, then slipped down and away from Fortune Hall. It might be many years before he saw her again. Perhaps they would never meet again.

He lifted the flap with his thumb-nail and slowly drew out the single sheet of notepaper. He scarcely knew what to expect as he unfolded it. It was short and direct and pain swept through him as he read the brief words.

"So now you despise me—but it won't last. I hope you'll try to understand—I think in time you will. Dear Luke—I'm sorry. "

For a long time he stared at the note. Then he pulled himself together and poured out a drink. He tossed the fiery liquid to the back of his throat. What was there to understand? Her behaviour of the previous night—no doubt she was used to men who appreciated her obvious desire for them and responded readily. She was a wanton who betrayed the fact with every sinuous movement, every intoxicating glance, every provocative smile. Yes, he despised her—and himself because he had almost surrendered to the call of his blood. She was sorry—why? For the attempted seduction? Or because she had come to Fortune Hall? Or did she know that he loved her and she was sorry it should be so? She was a strange woman and he had experienced her shrewd perception before —had she read in some chance expression, a casual remark, an instinctive gesture the truth that he had not dared to admit to himself until this morning?

Suddenly he crumpled the note in his hand and threw it across the room into a corner. Then he strode from the room and hurried up the wide staircase. Some ten minutes later, he left the house, immaculately dressed, and strode down the curving drive towards the gates. Life had to go on whether a love which was futile possessed him or not—and he was due to lunch at The Butts with Colonel Somers and his two daughters.

Maybe they thought him more cool and forbidding than usual or maybe he managed to hide his distraught emotions under a superficial veneer of easy charm and manner. He was indifferent to their thoughts.

After lunch he sat on the terrace with Margo Somers and he found her company strangely soothing. She was a tall fair young woman with china-blue eyes and a pink and white complexion. Her father called her his English rose and Luke, watching her fair head bent over a magazine, thought that the hackneyed phrase typified her. Her blonde hair was sleek and smooth and bound in a neat chignon at the back of her head. The sun caught it and gave it the lustre of gold. Her classic profile was turned to him and he thought how serene her expression was, how placid and smooth, as though her life was always untroubled by violent emotions or disturbances. She did not chatter—she made conversation when she thought her companion wanted to talk. If she sensed that he needed silence, then she was still and peaceful and quiet. They were very much at ease with each other. He had become friendly with the Colonel shortly after he moved to Fortune Hall and the two girls accepted him without question. He knew he was always welcome to appear at The Butts without invitation. He invariably went there when he was angry about something or when he was bored and lonely—for Margo had the power to soothe him by her very presence.

Now he compared her with Caprice—an unfair comparison for one was all disturbing vitality and the other was serene placidity. But where Margo could soothe him by her silent presence, Caprice could excite him with a glance from her dark eyes. He was very fond of Margo and her sister Lucille. Lucille was the livelier and she was invariably attended by some young man or another—so that Luke tended to turn to Margo for company when he was at The Butts. He knew that she was content with the state of affairs. He felt sure that she returned his mild and familiar affection. They shared many common interests and he found her to be intelligent as well as serene; he learned that she had a swift sense of humour which could quirk that sober mouth and lighten the contented blue eyes; he discovered that she possessed a warm sympathy and a rich fund of understanding.

Why had his heart decided to love Caprice when Margo was everything a man could want in a wife? Now he realised why he had hesitated to ask Margo to marry him during the last two years. She was so eminently suitable to be the mistress of Fortune Hall. Colonel Somers might not be very wealthy but he was descended from good family and there was breeding in every line of his two daughters and himself. But while he felt a warm and peaceful emotion towards Margo, he knew that Caprice lived in his blood and owned his heart. He could not give Margo all that she was entitled to as his wife, therefore he would leave matters as they were for the time being. Perhaps in time he would understand Caprice. Perhaps too he would eventually learn to live at peace with his love for her—and then he might feel that he could give Margo a certain amount of feeling and ask her to be his wife without the thought that he was being unfair to her or disloyal to himself.

Margo laid aside her magazine and lifted

her head. She smiled at Luke and said: "You have your sister-in-law staying with you, I believe? Why didn't you bring her to lunch?"

Luke stared at her for a moment. How did she know about Caprice? But the answer came to him instantly—the servants could not keep their tongues still and the knowledge that Caprice, Lady Veerham, had stayed overnight at Fortune Hall would be all over the village.

"Oh, it was just a flying visit," he said at last. "Caprice left this morning."

"Caprice?" she repeated. "What a delightful name! Is she beautiful, Luke? Did your brother keep up the family tradition of marrying a beauty?" The Somers were as knowledgeable on the Fortune history as he was himself and they had often discussed past Fortunes with interest, facts mingling with conjecture.

He took great care in the packing of his pipe with tobacco and then fiddled with matches and the tamping down of loose ends. At last, he looked up and said: "Beautiful? Caprice? Yes, I suppose she is. She came to tell me that she has assured the entail. She's going to have a child."

"That's good news!" Margo exclaimed. "She must be very happy."

"I imagine she'll be happier when she's more used to the idea," he said briefly. "Did you get your invitation to the Thwaites Ball yet, Margo? I received mine yesterday morning."

So he changed the subject and they went on to discuss the Thwaites and other acquaintances. Margo did not even notice that he had adroitly turned the conversation away from Lady Veerham. Although she exchanged remarks with him, her thoughts were busy and her heart was a little sad. She envied Lady Veerham —partly because she was happily married and partly because she was now expecting a child. Margo was in love with Luke Fortune and it seemed that everyone but he knew it. She longed to marry him and be the mistress of the lovely old Hall. She knew that her greatest joy would be to bear his children. She felt that her life would always be empty and futile if Luke did not soon realise that she wanted to be his wife. But she could not make it any clearer than she already had done. Her father had laughingly suggested that he have a word with Luke and demand to know his intentions. "After all, Margo, he's been hanging around you for two years. One imagines he means to marry you one day—but it seems so ridiculous to waste your lives in this fashion!"

"I don't think he even regards me in the light of a wife," she had replied quietly, evenly, while dark despair raged in her breast. "Please don't say anything, father."

It was becoming increasingly difficult not to openly betray her feelings and she knew that it could not be much longer before she voiced the love and hopes of her heart.

Luke took to visiting The Butts more and more frequently. He found certain solace for his loneliness in Margo's company and he did not realise the tumult that he roused within her. He looked upon her as a friend and companion.

Then one day, they were together at a dance held by the Master of the Hounds. They had hunted together earlier. That evening, Luke had called for Margo and escorted her to the dance. Lucille had an engagement of her own and the Colonel had cried off.

Margo looked quietly lovely in her gown of deep pink and her golden hair fell in a cascade of curls to the nape of her neck, fastened with a deep pink velvet band.

Luke stood by the staircase watching the dancers and he saw Margo swirl by in the arms of the Master's eldest son. She was laughing up at him, her skirts rustling and billowing, her golden hair bright in the lighting of the chandeliers, her slim and graceful body wrapped in the deep pink satin. He was vividly reminded of a portrait in the Picture Gallery at Veerham of an ancestress of his who had strayed from tradition and been born with a crop of golden curls—a honey-gold, richer than Margo's tresses—but her hair had been bound up in a similar style and this was enough similarity to stir Luke's memory. The shimmering, billowing satin brought to mind the many beautiful women in their sweeping gowns who had glided from room to room of Veerham and of Fortune Hall. Margo was beautiful too in a restful way—and it suddenly struck him with force that she would make him a pleasant and companionable wife. It was time now to ask her to marry him—and he could think of the prospect with a stirring of excitement.

He commandeered her as soon as the music ended and she was breathless and laughing. He wanted to take her into his arms and kiss the curving lips, the small and slender nose, the golden hair. Instead he caught her arm and said, "Let's slip into the library—I don't think there's anyone in there. I want to talk to you, Margo."

She went with him willingly and to his relief the room was empty. He went to the window and stood for a long moment, looking out. Now he would have to crush the thought of Caprice for ever. He had not seen her since her sudden descent on Fortune Hall and her equally swift departure. He knew that soon she would have her child and he felt that it was one more brick in the wall that he must erect between them. He was going to ask Margo to marry him—and when she was his wife, she would be entitled to a faithful husband —faithful in thought as well as in deed. It was no use to hanker for Caprice—but he knew his love was as vivid and as demanding as ever and just as uncrushable now as it had been several months ago.

She waited, puzzled by his long silence, then she went to his side and laid a questioning hand on his arm. He looked down at her gravely.

"What's wrong, Luke?" she asked quietly.

It was ridiculous that his courage should fail him now but he did not see a tall, blonde woman whose head was level with his chin—he looked down at a small, vital woman with glowing dark eyes and raven hair. He could feel the touch of her slim cool hands cradling his face and the soft fleeting pressure of cool lips on his. In his ears rang the sound of her husky voice, the lilt of her mocking laughter—and then he chased the phantom away by turning to Margo and placing his hands on her shoulders.

Very seriously, he said: "Margo, will you marry me? You've been very kind to me—I believe you're a little fond of me. I'm sure I can make you happy—so I'm just waiting for you to consent."

She met his eyes squarely. As ever, her

cool and serene expression did not betray the inner gladness, the swift joy, the instinctive prayer of thankfulness that her patience had been rewarded. In that moment she did not even realise that Luke's words had held nothing of love— all that mattered was that he had asked her to marry him and she knew that she would accept.

"I should like to marry you very much, Luke," she said. "If that is really what you want."

Luke did not know whether to laugh or groan at the matter of fact acceptance of a suggestion that had caused him no little pain or hesitancy. So he bent his head and kissed her lips—it was a kiss without passion, without love, a mere sealing of the contract.

By one of the odd coincidences of life, the announcement of their engagement was publicised in *The Times* on the same day as the announcement of the birth of a son, Adam Francis, to Caprice, Lady Veerham.

Luke's eyes were riveted to the small paragraph and then, with a sigh, he laid aside the newspaper with the full knowledge that he also laid aside the memory of something wonderful, rich and desirable, and completely beyond his reach.

Margo looked up at the sound of that brief sigh and her eyes were troubled. She had thought over his abrupt proposal many times and since she had realised that he had not told her that he loved her. He was kind and attentive, as always, but his kisses lacked warmth and she sensed that he was not as happy as a man about to marry should be. She went over to him and picked up the newspaper, scanning the announcements again. She saw the item which heralded the new heir to Veerham and she said quickly: "Oh, look, my dear, your brother's wife has had a son."

"Yes, I know," he replied flatly.

She regarded him through the long veil of her fair lashes. "You're not very attached to your brother, are you?"

He looked up at her. "Not particularly. Why?"

"It seems strange that you should know nothing about his child until it's announced in *The Times*. Didn't you expect that he would telephone you, at least?"

He shrugged. "Cliff wouldn't expect me to be interested, my dear Margo."

She pulled thoughtfully at her lower lip. "You will invite them to the wedding of course. Will you ask Cliff to act as your best man?" They had decided to be married quite soon and Margo was already concerning herself with the many arrangements and drawing up a list of guests.

Luke shook his head. "No. I thought I'd ask Barry Sylvester—or maybe one of my cousins. Invite them to the wedding by all means, Margo—but don't expect them to come. Cliff hates social occasions and he'll probably be abroad somewhere. He's a great traveller," and the last words were spoken with a trace of bitterness.

She laid a hand on his shoulder. "Luke, you do want to marry me?" Her voice trembled a little.

He quickly caught her hand in his. "Yes, of course I do." He smiled up at her. "What's wrong, my dear—you haven't changed your mind?"

"No," she replied swiftly, passionately. Then she bent over him and kissed him fleetingly on the lips. "I thought you would never ask me to marry you, darling."

He was startled by the passion in her voice and the warmth of her swift caress. He replied smoothly: "It takes me a long time to make up my mind—but once I've decided on my course of action I never swerve from it." There was more meaning than she could guess at in his words. He had made up his mind to erase the love for Caprice from his heart and thoughts, to marry Margo and make her happy, to be a loyal and faithful husband and keep the honour of the Fortunes intact.

She knelt down by his chair and clung to his hand. She studied his expression intently. "You do love me, Luke?"

He caught her close and buried his lips against the golden hair. "What a question? Of course I do." And it was true. He loved Margo with none of the burning passion in his blood that his love for Caprice brought but with a quiet love that he told himself would be the more lasting. Margo would make him a good wife: undemanding, peaceful and satisfactory; he would never know the heights of ecstacy, the incessant yearning and desire, the painful need which was his love for Caprice, but in the same way that he had forgone Veerham and made himself content with Fortune Hall, so he would forgo his dreams of Caprice and make himself content with Margo. She loved Fortune Hall and Mallingham: she was familiar with and well liked by the people who lived on the estate; she was well-bred, intelligent and beautiful—a most suitable wife for him in every way. He could rely on her affection and loyalty. He appreciated her loveliness and her companionship. He knew that she was fond of him as he was fond of her—he was blind to the passion which lay deep in her being and the all-consuming love she knew for him: Margo sensed this even while he held her close and deep within she was sad. There was a core of determination in the apparently serene Margo and it was then that she decided to win Luke's love—even if it took her the rest of her life. For the present, she knew that he was very fond of her, that he loved her a little and was happy in her company, that he would be a good husband to the best of his ability

—and she contented herself with this even while she longed for some sign of passion and warmth from him.

5

THREE months later, Luke Fortune married Margo Somers in the small and ancient church of St. Peter's in Mallingham. It was a fashionable wedding and over two hundred guests squeezed into the small church for the ceremony.

To Luke's surprise, Cliff had accepted the invitation to the wedding. They arrived late and Luke, standing with his cousin, Lionel Fortune, his best man, was immediately aware that Caprice had entered the church. He had not seen her entry. He did not look back in search of her. But the prickling of the hair on the back of his neck, the dryness of his mouth, the tension of his nerves and the sudden racing of his heart all told him that the woman he loved had come to see him married to Margo.

It was the first time that Cliff and Caprice had come to Mallingham together. Caprice knew nothing of his unexpected visit to the Hall while she was in Cornwall:

Cliff knew nothing of his wife's overnight stay with his brother while he was abroad. They left their son, Adam, in the care of his nurse and drove from Veerham to Mallingham, stopping overnight at a small but comfortable hotel en route.

Cliff did not attempt to conceal his amusement that his brother should be entering the matrimonial state. He had made several mocking comments during the drive to Mallingham and Caprice had made but brief replies. When, however, Cliff had remarked that Luke would soon regret it as much as he had, then Caprice had lost her temper and they had argued bitterly.

She had been reluctant to attend the wedding but Cliff had insisted that Luke was his only brother and while he detested him, it was his duty to be present to give him moral support for the ordeal ahead— this last with an ironic chuckle for Cliff had never allowed duty to interfere with his wishes. Their life together was not easy these days for Caprice had spoken truly when she told Luke that once he had married her, Cliff's interest waned and he now sought other women to stir his blood.

He had never been content until he owned a beautiful thing—but once it was his, he was no longer concerned about it. It surprised Caprice now that she had managed to hold his affections for so many years before she became his wife—but even then she had known him to be unfaithful to her whenever the opportunity or the desire arose. Her love for him was as though it had never been and only Adam reconciled her to being Cliff's wife. She adored her son passionately if it seemed to others that she accepted his existence with casual indifference. It had always been her nature to hide her deep emotions with a superficial barrier of mocking amusement. Adam was a healthy child with the Fortune hair and features, which were definite even at so young an age. He showed already that he was temperamental and wilful and there were times when Caprice prayed with real fervour that he should have inherited more of the Fortune qualities than those of the Cliffords which were so strong in her husband. Cliff took little interest in his son. As far as he was concerned, the heir to Veerham was now assured and that had been his only motive in giving Caprice a child. He enjoyed being Lord Veerham, and the arrogance which in Luke was a natural facet of his character was a little overdone because of its adoption in Cliff. He was very much Lord of the Manor when he was at Veerham and this earned Caprice's contempt. To her relief, he was away more than he was at Veerham—and she had settled down happily in her new home, making only the occasional visit to London, and finding new friends in the district who liked her but did not understand her, accepting her for her position and her charm and her warm vitality.

Now Caprice sat beside Cliff in one of the pews and her eyes burned into Luke's back as he stood waiting for his bride. He had not noticed their entry. He did not turn to scan the guests to discover if his brother had yet arrived. He seemed perfectly at his ease, as he talked in low tones to his best man, and she wondered about the woman who was so soon to be his wife. How tall and well-built he was: how the sun fell on his hair and caused it to gleam redly; how firm and clean-looking was the nape of his neck. She might almost have been looking at her husband but there was a subtle difference about Luke Fortune which even the most casual observer must surely appreciate.

There was a rustle of murmurs throughout the church and then the organ, which had been playing softly, broke into Mendelssohn's Wedding March.

Then it was that Luke turned and as he did so, he met Caprice's eyes. Their gaze held but briefly and then she smiled in greeting—a rich, slow smile. He dragged his eyes away and watched his bride come slowly down the aisle on the Colonel's arm, a vision of gold and white, radiant and serene, a tremulous smile just touching her lips. He smiled a response and held out his hand to her. Their hands met and clasped, then they turned to the altar and the ceremony began.

He forced out the thought of Caprice and tried to concentrate on the service which seemed long and yet too swift. His responses were clear and firm as though he impressed upon Caprice that this was the end of anything that might have existed between them.

Cliff touched Caprice's arm and

murmured in her ear: "I admire his taste —I rather expected some horse-faced old hag . . ." The rest of his words were lost as the congregation began to sing one of the hymns chosen for the service.

Caprice did not reply and she did not even glance at her husband. She was thinking of her own hurried wedding in a registrar's office in Perth and of Cliff's obvious distaste for the whole business. She wondered again—as she had wondered so many times—why he had ever married her. Was it simply because he wanted to prove to the world that she was his possession and no other man must look at her? Or had he feared, even if briefly, that he might lose her—and no man must take anything from him to which he had laid claim? Or had it been an impulse—a quickening of emotion which for the time being he had chosen to call love? Caprice felt that she would never know—and after all, she was not much interested. One day, she supposed, they would separate—their marriage was beyond repair now. But with this thought came the fear that he might insist on taking Adam away from her and she knew that come what may she would bear with any humiliation or unhappiness in order to keep Adam close to her.

It was over and Margo was his wife. Luke led her into the small vestry and there they both signed the register. Congratulations and kisses followed—and lastly the triumphant walk down the aisle and from the church. Once again, he met Caprice's eyes and there was mockery in her glittering glance. A brief touch of amusement as if she assured him that although he might have married another woman he could never forget her and all his life a mere glance, a word or a touch could quicken his pulse.

An open carriage waited for them outside the church and he lifted Margo into it while the guests pelted them with rose-petals and confetti. As the carriage drove away, he glanced down at Margo and found her eyes shining with laughter and happiness.

He caught her hand and pressed it. "I suppose women love all this fuss and ceremony? I could have done without it."

She threw him a reproachful glance. "Darling, I hate hole in the corner weddings. This is only the beginning—there's the reception to come."

He groaned in mock dismay. "I shall be glad to get away from it all and have you to myself, Margo." They were going to Italy for a month's honeymoon.

She smiled and lifted his hand to her lips. "I love you," she murmured with warmth in her eyes. "Even if you are a wet blanket!"

He bent his head to kiss her lips then she drew away, rearranging her lovely veil. "Later, darling," she promised. "I don't want to receive our guests looking untidy."

He thought briefly that Caprice would have eagerly returned that kiss and not given a thought to her appearance—but he dismissed the disloyal thought as swiftly as it was born. Margo, not Caprice, was his wife.

Cliff heartily slapped his shoulder and shook his hand. "Congratulations, Luke! May I kiss the bride?" He smiled at Margo. "I'm your brother-in-law so you can't object."

She laughed. "I couldn't mistake your

identity, Cliff—you and Luke are too alike."

"Only in looks," he returned lightly. "I'm the gay buccaneer—Luke's the stick-in-the-mud of the present generation." He caught her close and kissed her full on the mouth with more warmth than the occasion merited. She released herself with a brief protest.

Caprice, standing a little to one side, threw her husband a contemptuous glance. Then she held out a small hand to Luke. "I hope you'll be happy," she said softly, huskily.

Her hand was cool and clinging in his and he was reluctant to release it. At last she withdrew it but the gesture was lingering. "Thank you, Caprice," he said. "I'm glad you and Cliff came."

"We were very late," she offered lightly. "But Cliff always leaves things till the last moment."

"How is Adam?" he asked politely.

"Oh, thriving." She dismissed the subject of her son. She turned to Margo who was adjusting her wispy coronet. "My dear, you look lovely—and the ceremony was charming. I hope you'll be happy."

They were the same words she had used to Luke but there was a world of difference in her tone—and then Luke realised that when she addressed them to him there had been the implication that she doubted very much if he could content himself with the woman he had chosen for his wife.

"You're Caprice, of course," Margo said swiftly. She leaned forward and kissed the woman's cheek with light affection. "I've heard so much about you from Luke—I'm sorry you couldn't stay long enough to join us for lunch when you stayed here some time ago."

Caprice answered shortly, "It was only a flying visit." She had noticed Cliff's expression of enquiry and she was annoyed. Luke too was annoyed that Margo had mentioned Caprice's visit but for a different reason. It would seem that he frequently mentioned Caprice to Margo but he had hardly mentioned her name since that visit so many months ago.

Cliff and Caprice left them and went in search of a drink. He looked after them and noticed that Caprice was as slim as ever despite her new maternity. She walked with the same lithe grace and vitality flowed with every movement from her slim body.

Margo followed the direction of his eyes. "She *is* lovely," she said a little ungraciously. "She doesn't look in the least like the mother of a baby son."

Luke laughed. "Don't sound so disappointed, darling. Come on, we'd better circulate a little." He put his hand on her arm and smiled down at her. Her eyes were troubled for a moment then she returned his smile.

"I'm being silly—but it seemed that there was something between you and Caprice—just a feeling I had. I felt like an outsider—and I didn't like it."

"My dear, you're imagining things. I never met Caprice until she'd been married to Cliff for two years. We'd better detach Lionel from that pretty sister of yours—as the best man he's supposed to distribute his charms among all the guests." She quickly forgot the momentary feeling but Luke did not forget her words. He realised too that the swift reassurance had held a lie. It was not strictly true that he had not met Caprice until after she became Cliff's wife—but the lie was justified in his eyes if it soothed the twinge of jealousy which Margo had felt.

He lost sight of Margo for a few minutes during the reception and assumed that she was surrounded by a group of friends, all eager to hear the exciting details of her wedding finery and the arrangements for the honeymoon. He was standing alone, a glass of champagne in his hand, a little away from his guests and watching them with a detached expression. For the moment, it seemed that this was not his wedding day: that he was still as free as ever; that his first concern in the future would not be Margo, his wife.

"You look like a man who's just dived from the high board and then discovered that he cannot swim," an amused voice said behind him.

He spun round and found Caprice close to him. "Do I?" he returned. "I admit this is all a little overwhelming."

She was lovely in an exquisitely-tailored suit. The deep flame colour enhanced her dark, glowing beauty. Her skin was a creamy velvet: her full mouth moist and sensuous; her dark eyes full of amusement.

"I don't suppose you'd tell me why you

married that charming but cold woman. In fact, you wouldn't admit that you're not in love with her, would you?"

He said curtly: "You're leaping to conclusions."

She laughed softly. "I'm just perceptive, my dear. I hope this marriage is more of a success than mine—but I suppose it contains all the ingredients for success. She's a determined young woman—and you're the faithful type. Which is more than I can say for your charming brother." Her voice held contempt.

"You really aren't happy with him?" he asked with concern.

Her eyes laughed at him. "Did you really think that my remarks were merely the fancy of an expectant mother? Dear Luke. You really don't know me very well."

"I don't know you at all," he reminded her. "I've seen you—what, three, four times—in several years—briefly at that. You can't expect me to know you."

"But I know you, Luke," she said firmly.

He shrugged. "So you imagine."

She ignored this. "Well, I expect Margo

will make you an admirable wife. She'll always do the right thing at the right moment—she'll probably present you with a couple of healthy children who'll be brought up to do the right thing at the right moment. She'll make an excellent hostess when you entertain. She'll run your home and your life equally well. She'll accept all your lordly dictums without protest and turn you into a well-behaved and dull husband."

Anger flooded him swiftly. "At least she'll always be faithful to me."

Her eyes burned. "And you think I'm not faithful to Cliff? Worse things can happen to a marriage, Luke. I prophesy that you'll be bored to death with each other within a few years—I may annoy Cliff, I may merit his dislike and contempt —but I never bore him." Her temper waned suddenly. "He bores me to death —but if I were married to you, I don't think you'd bore me, Luke." She surveyed him thoughtfully for a moment. "I'd never turn you into a well-behaved husband, my dear—in fifty years you would still be my lover and that I think is the secret of a happy marriage."

He glanced at his watch. "You'll have to excuse me, Caprice. I must find Margo."

"The bonds begin to tighten," she said mockingly. "And you run away from the truth of my words—well, I don't blame you. Most men run from the truth." She sighed briefly. "I expect Cliff is thoroughly bored with this affair by now—unless he's found an attractive woman who is equally attracted by him. I think it's time we made our farewells." She smiled up at him. "May I kiss you, Luke?" Before he replied, she had cupped his face in her hands. Before her lips could touch his, he put his hands up and grasped her wrists. Then he moved away from her.

"You've kissed me too often, Caprice," he said harshly. Their eyes met and held for a long moment. Then she nodded. "Yes, I think that is the trouble."

He turned on his heel and strode away and she looked after him with a slow smile curving her lips and an enigmatic gleam in her eyes.

That night he held Margo in his arms. She was light, almost ethereal in her loveliness, and she was half-asleep. Passion was spent and he had been astonished at the depth of passion in this woman who had always seemed to be cool and undisturbed by emotion. He recalled that Caprice had called her cold—and a smile touched his eyes.

Margo raised a hand to touch his cheek and then followed the line of his lips in the darkness. He kissed her finger-tips and she sighed happily.

"No regrets?" he murmured, turning so his lips were against her small, shell-like ear.

She laughed lightly. "Ask me again in fifty years' time," she told him. "Luke, we're going to be so happy—I know it."

"Of course we are," he returned and he caught her close, so that he could feel her heart-beat beneath the flimsy nightdress she wore.

Soon, he knew that she slept and he listened to the quiet evenness of her breathing. Her hair was silky and sweet-smelling, curling about his throat as she lay in his arms, her head on his shoulder. He knew that he envied her sweet surrender to the cloak of sleep—for it eluded him and he lay on his back, his eyes open staring into the darkness and hearing in the background the small sounds which told him that London never slept.

The future stretched before him and he was sure that Margo represented a serene happiness, a promise of contentment.

She was everything that a man could wish—and she was his wife. There was a certain pride in his thoughts as he repeated those words. Margo was his wife.

Yet, unbidden, came the remembrance of Caprice and he could not still the uneven tempo of his heart, the wild longing. Was he always to feel the power of her spell? She had bewitched him and bound him to her—and she knew it and laughed at his weakness. She was a devil in feminine form—temptation in every line of her body, every glance of those fascinating eyes. She was a woman with mysterious depths and he knew that she had spoken truthfully when she told him that Cliff was never bored with her even if their marriage was a failure. She could stir any man's emotions with one wicked glance, one graceful movement of her lovely body. She was the kind of woman to bring fear to the hearts of other women and the impulse to guard their husbands carefully. She was provocative and exciting and beautiful—she knew all these things and exercised her charms deliberately. To know that a man was caught in her spell was probably meat and drink to her. If a man ever admitted that she had won him, then she would never release him and all his life he would be tormented by her mysterious power.

But he loved her. This was such a love as came only once in a man's lifetime and he was well and truly fettered. Useless to fight against the compulsion of his blood. Even the defence of marriage was no defence against the cry of his heart. Margo was sweet and lovely and he could be proud to call her his wife—but Caprice was the woman he loved with all his being. In fifty years' time he would love her still and the force of his love would flow as strongly within him.

He was flooded with hatred for Cliff who did not value his possession of Caprice except in the casual way he valued any beautiful possession and considered that he had the right to own it. Caprice had been born for love and happiness and

Cliff denied her these things. How could she be blamed for seeking them elsewhere —and he knew instinctively that she would go on seeking to assuage her need. It was strange that Cliff should have captivated her affections in the first place and then held them all those years before she married him. But he did not deny that Cliff possessed a certain charm which was attractive to women. Perhaps his very reluctance to marry her had been an attraction—kindling a determination to be his wife eventually at no matter what cost. Well, she had succeeded and he knew that there was regret on both sides. Cliff was essentially a man who valued his freedom and Caprice needed a man who would never tire of her and to whom she would always come first before anything else.

As he lay thinking thus of Caprice, he realised that he did know and understand her as any man who really loved her could know and understand her. He was filled with sudden pity for her loneliness, the desperate need for happiness, the conflicting and turbulent emotions which battled within her.

A beautiful woman born with the knowledge of that beauty and power it brought her. Ensnared in the net of her own capacity for passion and warmth and married to a man who did not appreciate her need and was fool enough to look for his own happiness outside his marriage.

He loved Caprice. But he had married Margo and his first duty was to her, his first consideration always her welfare and happiness, his first loyalty to the girl he had made his wife. It would be a difficult road to travel, constantly suppressing the longing for Caprice and denying the love in his heart for her, yet never failing to prove to Margo that he loved her and wanted to make her happy.

For he loved Margo too. It seemed ridiculous on the face of it but it was true. As she lay asleep in his arms, he felt a surge of tenderness, the longing to protect her from the knowledge that he loved Caprice more, and a warm tide of affection for the woman that she was and would prove to be. He did not know if he could always live with the secret safe in his heart —women were so quick to sense these things—but he knew that he would do all in his power to keep it safe.

6

LUKE leaned back in his chair and regarded his cousin Lionel. He thought that Lionel was beginning to show his age. His hair was receding a little and his pleasant face had thickened about the chin. Abruptly, he realised that only a few years separated their ages and no doubt he was beginning to age a little. He put up a hand and brushed his hair back, cautiously, as though he fully expected to find its thickness waning. But it was still thick and waving strongly in its red-gold mass.

Lionel said, offering his cigarette case across the table, "Well, we don't see much of you in London these days, Luke. But you never did like city life."

Luke took a cigarette with a nod of thanks. "Give me the country life any day. You're looking well and prosperous, Lionel—as busy as ever, I suppose."

"Yes, indeed." He grinned. "My side of the family was never as fortunate as yours," and the pun was deliberate. "I've sunk most of my income into the business and now it's paying off, thank goodness."

"You'll tell me next that you've never been able to afford a wife," Luke said tightly.

"That's not strictly true, if you mean financially. I've never been able to afford the time for marriage—and I believe wives are a full-time occupation." He busied himself with a lighter which was obstinate. At last it spun into life and he leaned across the restaurant table towards Luke who inclined his head over the flame. "Margo isn't with you, Luke?"

Luke had come to London for a few days on business. Colonel Somers had recently died leaving Margo money and property and Luke was investigating the state of the property for his wife. It had occurred to him that a meeting with his cousin would be pleasant for they had not seen each other for over a year. Lionel was a hearty and likeable type and the family ties were strong even though time might pass between meetings.

"No, not this time." He shook his head briefly.

"I'm sorry about her father—you'll give her my sympathies, won't you?"

"She's taken it very well," Luke said. "But I think she and the Colonel drifted apart a little during the last few years. Margo's always so wrapped up in domestic affairs—the house, entertaining friends, the children . . ."

"How are the children?"

"Both very well now. Francesca had measles but it doesn't seem to have left any ill-effects."

"She always was the delicate one, I remember," Lionel said. "The other one —Serena—she's a bonny child, isn't she?"

"Yes. Serena's very healthy." He spoke with certain pride. Of his two daughters, Serena was the one he loved with all his heart. It had always seemed that Serena was more his child and Francesca belonged to Margo.

"They're lucky to be growing up at Mallingham," Lionel said with a brief sigh. "Do you remember the old days when we were all kids together, Luke? God, it's so many years ago that I prefer not to recall them too often."

He rambled on, interspersing his words

with many "do you remembers" and Luke nodded and agreed and inwardly itched to leave his cousin. The past was best forgotten for there were too many memories in the past for him. He listened with half an ear to his cousin but he was thinking of Margo and their marriage. Eight years. It could almost be yesterday that he had married her—and they had been happy. Happier than he had thought possible on their wedding night when he had been tormented with longing for Caprice even while Margo lay in his arms. Margo had been a wonderful wife. They had two lovely daughters and he had welcomed them both. Serena was the youngest and she would be five next month. Francesca at seven was the image of Margo—tall and slender and golden-haired. But Serena—how ill the name suited her for there was nothing serene about his tempestuous daughter. She was mischievous and excitable and utterly adorable. The red-gold hair of the Fortunes fell to her waist in a silken mass: her eyes were deep blue and full of laughter; she would be tall for her legs were long and straight but she already had the bearing and poise of the Fortunes. His love for her was sometimes so strong that it brought him pain for he knew that one day she would turn from the father she adored and give all her passionate kisses and impulsive caresses to the man she would love. Francesca was a strangely self-sufficient child—but so was Margo and she had inherited that from her. She was patient and reserved. Her kisses were few and far between and she followed her own pursuits. It seemed that she did not need anyone and he wondered if it would always be so.

Margo had that cool reserve. Sometimes he wondered if she had found him strangely lacking as a husband and turned her thoughts and emotions inwards. She was a loyal wife and he knew that she loved him but after Serena's birth she had withdrawn from him some of the old warmth and passion which had always been his. She was his wife now and the mother of his children—and sometimes he felt that he had lost a lover who had once been generous with her affection. He still loved her as he had always done—a quiet, sweet emotion with none of the fire of his love for Caprice.

His thoughts often turned to Caprice. They did so now and he tried to remember when he had last seen her. The bond between him and Cliff, weak as it had always been, seemed non-existent after their separate marriages. Once or twice, casually, he had turned up at the Hall, Caprice and Adam with him, but they had been brief visits. Once, he had taken Margo and the two girls to Veerham and they had stayed with Cliff and Caprice for two weeks. Margo had thought Veerham beautiful but lacking in the warmth and friendliness of the Hall—and he had found that he was disappointed for he had never lost his passionate devotion to Veerham. It was nearly two years now since Cliff's last visit to Mallingham and he had read somewhere or other that he had gone to America again shortly after, taking Caprice with him and leaving his son in the capable care of a nurse. As far as he knew, they were still over there but he thought it unlikely that Caprice would leave Adam for so long. He had seen her with the child and wondered at her possessive pride in him. It had seemed to him that she was continually weaning his affections from his father and he wondered if it were deliberate.

At last, Lionel rose reluctantly. "I'm sorry it's been such a brief meeting, Luke," he said, "but duty calls and I must get back to the gallery." Art had always been the one passion of his life and he was the owner of a small art gallery in Bond Street which was very successful.

With the rueful thought that the meal had not taken up such a brief period of time, Luke rose too and the two men shook hands. "I'll have some more coffee before I leave," Luke said. "It was nice to see you, Lionel."

His cousin smiled. "I wish we saw more of each other—but I don't get much time for holidays."

"You must come down to Mallingham and spend a few weeks soon," Luke said warmly. "Margo will be delighted to see you—and the girls are very fond of you."

"Thanks—I'll try to do that. Give my love to Margo and those two bewitching imps—and I won't forget Serena's birthday next month."

Luke sat down again as Lionel strode purposefully through the restaurant. No, he wouldn't forget, Luke thought. His cousin was a kindly man and always remembered to send small but expensive gifts on birthdays and at Christmas. He was generous and warm-hearted and very fond of Luke's daughters who always welcomed him with open arms. It occurred to Luke that Francesca's welcome was tempered with a mercenary interest in what he might have brought for her but Serena's passionate welcome was whole-hearted and she would not care if his pockets were empty. This typified the difference in his two daughters: Francesca was cool, practical and resolute; Serena was warm and reckless and easily diverted —unless she had set her heart on one thing and then she never swerved from her determination to own it.

It seemed a pity that Lionel had never married for he was what Luke called a family man. But love and marriage and children would never attract him from his main interest—art.

He called for his bill and, opening his wallet, threw down some notes on the tray.

As the waiter thanked him deferentially and turned to leave, Luke rose. But a light hand on his shoulder caused him to turn. "Don't run away yet, Luke," a well-remembered voice said lightly. "This is a chance encounter indeed. I've been lunching alone—I wouldn't disturb you and Lionel—I'm afraid I find him rather a bore." Caprice slipped into the chair that Lionel had recently vacated and smiled warmly across the table.

"I didn't know you were in London," he said, striving for composure while her very touch had brought about a tumult within him.

"And I thought you were buried deep in the heart of the country," she returned. She looked deep into his eyes. "How nice it is to see you," she said and the words were almost a sigh. She was looking immaculate as ever in a white sheath dress with an immense ruby brooch catching up the folds at her breast. It matched the ruby which glittered on her engagement finger —a big ring which almost covered the wide band of her wedding ring. Over her dress she wore a light coat, loose and flowing, of the same colour and material as her dress. Her jet black hair cascaded about her small head and though her eyes glittered with the familiar vitality there was a hint of sadness in their depths and he noticed that her mouth showed that all was not well with her happiness. He wondered briefly how old she was now. She looked scarcely older than the first time he had met her at the Croesus theatre and that was more years ago than he cared to remember.

"You're looking very well," he said formally.

She smiled slowly, banishing the discontent from her lips. "Once you would have said I was looking beautiful," she said lightly. "But the years are not kind to anyone—least of all a woman."

He leaned forward and placed his hand over the slender, restless fingers. "You are looking beautiful—but I didn't see why I should pander to your vanity."

She studied him intently. "And you're looking exceptionally handsome—I rather like those threads of silver at your temples, Luke. Most distinguished."

He laughed. He was suddenly at ease with her, grateful for this chance to talk to her. He realised how many years it was since he had been alone with her and not known the fear that he would give away his inner emotions while others were present. He felt that it would not matter any more if she knew without doubt that he loved her—but he did not have any intention of telling her so. It really wasn't necessary, he knew, as their eyes met across the table. She had known eight years ago that he loved her and she knew that it was the bright flame which could never be extinguished.

"How's Adam?" he asked eagerly, wanting to show her that he knew that Adam was the most important person in her life.

She returned the pressure of his fingers. "He's in fine form—I'm terribly proud of him, Luke. Sometimes I wonder how Cliff and I ever managed to produce such an intelligent and worthwhile individual." She added huskily, "I'm glad you didn't ask about Cliff. But in order to relieve your mind, he's very well and as dissolute as ever. He grows more pompous and self-opinionated with every passing day."

Luke felt a momentary embarrassment

at the cold contempt in her voice. He said abruptly: "Do you ever try to make anything of your marriage, Caprice? There was something between you once. If only for Adam's sake."

She replied coolly: "Not even for Adam's sake. Dear Luke. You're as naïve as ever. Cliff and I have a mutual agreement—to detest each other and to lead our own lives. If it wasn't for Adam, we'd have broken up years ago."

It was wonderful to hear that familiar endearment on her lips again. Many times, in the night when he lay restless and despondent, longing for Caprice, he had fancied that he heard her say in that light, affectionate tone: *"Dear Luke"*. Many times, he went over in his mind the many occasions when she had applied the endearment and knew it was only when she was tenderly laughing at him.

"What are you doing in London?" he asked, stiffly, deciding to ignore her remarks on her husband and her marriage.

She shrugged. "Trying to relieve the monotony of my existence. Cliff is entertaining some of his unpleasant friends at Veerham and I couldn't stand it any longer

—so I made some flimsy excuse to get away. I'm staying at the flat and I'm finding that one is bored no matter where one is. I think boredom must be a disease of the soul."

"I can't imagine you being bored with anything," he said warmly. "You're such a vital person, Caprice."

She looked at him lazily from half-closed eyes and he noticed absently the incredible length of her curving dark lashes. "When do you go back to Mallingham?"

He shrugged slightly. "In a few days. I want to find something nice for Serena—she's five next month, you know. And I've a few friends to look up. One tends to lose touch when one sees little of one's friends."

"I shall be in London until the end of the week. Perhaps we could see something of each other?" There was a note of invitation in her voice and her eyes glowed with the old provocation as she leaned forward eagerly.

He longed to agree, to demand that all her waking hours for the next few days should be spent with him, to snatch at the opportunities which this chance encounter had brought about. But he hesitated.

Her eyes mocked him then. "How you must love your fetters, Luke! Why not loosen them for a few days? Life is too short to miss up the chance of happiness."

He said curtly: "What are you offering me, Caprice? Not simply a few hours of companionship, the occasional meal together, a theatre perhaps, I'm convinced." He glanced at her and to his surprise saw swift pain flash across her expression. Then she swiftly gathered up her bag and gloves. Before she could rise to her feet, he caught her hand. "Forgive me," he said quietly.

She searched his eyes and read the very real contrition in their depths. Then she smiled and caressed the back of his hand with her cool fingers. "Leaping to conclusions was always one of your faults, Luke. But there's nothing to forgive—I don't blame you for thinking me immoral. This will surprise you—but I've never been actually unfaithful to Cliff—only in thought and desire. For the simple reason that only one man could bring it about— and he just isn't the type."

He did not realise then that she referred to him. He was so utterly taken by surprise by her words. He had never believed that she was loyal to his brother. Many years ago he had understood her capacity for passion and forgiven her readily for any unfaithfulness she might indulge in. How generous he had been, he mocked himself, forgiving this woman for a crime she had never committed if he could believe her now. And how easily he had deceived himself that he was incapable of betraying Cliff when he knew full well that he would gladly have done so if Caprice had given him the chance.

The restaurant was crowded and the hum of conversation rose in what seemed like a crescendo to Luke. He said abruptly: "Let's get out of here, Caprice —unless you'd like some coffee?"

She shook her head. "I've finished lunch." She rose obediently and preceded him from the restaurant.

It was a fresh Spring day and the sun was high overhead. It brought a touch of warmth to the bleak buildings of the city. They walked along the busy streets and Caprice linked her hand in his arm with a casual movement. It disturbed him that her touch should have such a devastating effect on his emotions. He knew that he was grateful for this opportunity to be with her. He knew that he was glad of her presence, of her hand on his arm, of the knowledge that he was in love with her as much now as ever.

"We're walking aimlessly," she said lightly.

He looked down at her. Her head barely reached his shoulder and he compared her with Margo's slim height and cool assurance. He felt briefly that this woman was strangely disturbed because he walked by her side—she seemed completely at her ease and yet he sensed that her heart was pounding and the blood flowed swiftly in her veins. He said abruptly: "You're staying at the flat?"

"Yes. Let's go there. I want to talk to you—to hear about the girls—and to talk about Adam. Cliff is never interested in him and no one understands how I feel about my son—except you, Luke."

He hailed a passing taxi without comment. They sat apart, too conscious of each other, not even daring to let their hands touch. It seemed too soon and yet an eternity before the taxi drew up outside a big block of flats. He did not let his thoughts dwell on what might happen when they were alone. But he felt instinctively that he would need all his self-control and he tried to concentrate his thoughts on Margo and his daughters as he sat so close and so apart from Caprice.

This had been the flat which Cliff had taken when he first left Veerham and he had kept it on for it was conveniently situated and very useful as a centrepoint for his visits to London. Luke had been there before but as he entered the big lounge and looked about him he noted subtle improvements in the decor and furnishings and correctly attributed them to Caprice's taste and influence.

Caprice slipped out of her loose coat and left him for a moment with a brief word of excuse. When she returned, he was sitting on a deep settee, leaning forward, hands loosely linked between his knees, and his eyes were on a framed sketch of her which hung over the mantelpiece. It was cleverly done and the artist had obviously captured her in a bewitching mood.

"Cliff did that," she volunteered.

He looked his surprise. "Cliff?"

"Yes. He does have a few talents, you know." He thought that she seemed a little nervous. "It's too early for tea—would you like a drink, Luke?"

"No, thanks."

"A cigarette then." She indicated the box on the low table and he helped himself. She picked up a table lighter and flicked it into life. As she held it towards him, he saw that her hand was shaking a little. She did not take a cigarette herself. She sat down beside him on the settee, a little apart. "Tell me about the girls," she invited. "They're attractive little beggars. What are they now—seven and five, I suppose?"

"Serena's five next month. Francesca is seven."

She fingered her lower lip thoughtfully. "Oh yes. Francesca is the one who takes after Margo—and Serena resembles you."

Eagerly he began to speak of his daughters, not realising how his voice softened and took on a tender note when he spoke of Serena.

She said: "You feel about Serena as I

feel about Adam. He's wholly mine, you know. I sometimes think that I managed to produce him by myself—fortunately he hasn't inherited any of Cliff's traits." She indicated a framed photograph which stood on a piano by the window. "That was taken recently—it's very good, isn't it?"

Luke rose and crossed to examine it. He saw a sturdy child with a mop of bright curls and eyes that glowed with vitality. His features were good, handsome and sober. He was standing with his hands thrust into his pockets and he held himself arrogantly, Luke noticed.

"He's an odd mixture," Caprice went on lightly. "Cliff's hair and my eyes—he's going to be very handsome. He'll break a lot of hearts, I think."

He turned to the piano and lifted the lid. He ran his fingers across the keys and the notes were sweet and tender. "Do you play?" he asked and he realised how little he knew about Caprice—the everyday things, her likes and dislikes, her talents, were all unknown to him.

"Yes," she said. She came to stand beside him and the perfume of her hair was in his nostrils. Desire flooded him and he moved away slightly. She sat down at the piano and began to play softly, melodiously, a tune he liked. She did not look at her hands. She was looking at him and her eyes were frank. He realised that all trace of nervousness was gone. She was once again sure of herself and of her power and he was incapable of tearing his eyes away from her compelling gaze. "Do you know what this is called?" she asked quietly.

He nodded. "Yes, it used to be a favourite of mine."

"Time cannot change my love for you," she quoted lightly and then she began to sing the familiar words. Her voice was husky, attractive and musical. She sang it through to the end and then continued to play the melody. "It deepens with every passing year," she said softly, quoting again. Suddenly she slammed her hands down on the keys, harsh discord taking the place of the lovely tune. "How the years pass!" she exclaimed bitterly. "Lonely, empty years." Luke glanced at her sharply, startled. "Have you ever been lonely?" she asked wearily. "I don't mean physically—but spiritually alone?"

He leaned across to knock the ash from his cigarette into an ashtray which stood on the piano top. In doing so, his hand lightly brushed her shoulder and he both felt and saw a tremor run through her slight body. "No, I don't think so," he replied slowly yet he knew what she meant. "I'm a self-sufficient person, I think."

She laughed softly. "I like to think I am too—but it isn't true. I depend on Adam to a very great extent. If I had married more wisely, I would depend on my husband even more." She said painfully: "You know that Cliff is determined to send Adam away to school next year?"

"He'll be nine—time he went to school," he told her but he knew that he could do nothing to ease the anguish in her heart. He tried to imagine how he would feel if Margo decided to send Serena away for two thirds of the year and he knew each parting would be a small death.

"My life will really be empty then," she said and it was the first time he had heard real sadness in her voice. Bitterness and contempt: amusement and mockery; indifference and fleeting pain. But never this wretched despair, this hint of future blackness.

He put his hands over hers as they lay still on the keyboard and he raised her until she was standing close to him. Then they looked into each other's eyes for a long moment. Reluctantly and yet unable to help himself, he bent his head and sought her lips, feeling them moist and cool beneath his mouth, catching the tiny sigh which escaped her and knowing that their breaths mingled as they kissed. She was very still but he felt her lips parting under the pressure of his eager touch and his love for her seemed to possess his entire being. He was not ashamed of the desire which leapt in him. He did not care that he openly revealed the force of his emotions. He only knew that her lips responded ardently and he forgot everything but the fulfilment of a wish which had lain always in his heart.

She was the first to draw away. Then she smiled at him and it was a very sweet, tender smile. "Dear Luke," she murmured. "Do you know that's the first time you've kissed me? I thought I should be for ever taking the initiative. No, don't kiss me again," as he would have drawn her close. "Let's talk about the children—it's safe ground."

So he moved away from her, though the effort cost him something, and she walked over to the settee and began to talk about Serena and Francesca and Adam as though that kiss had never been although its effect still lingered in his blood and he knew she was trembling.

When he left he said stiffly, "I'm sorry, Caprice—I had no right to kiss you."

She smiled. "No apologies, please. I'm glad you kissed me. May I see you tomorrow?"

He had invited her to dine with him that night and take in a show but she had pleaded a previous engagement and he knew she lied but he understood her motives.

So now he said: "Yes, of course. I'll telephone you in the morning." The door closed behind him and he walked thoughtfully to the lift.

7

HE spent the evening alone. He was racked with guilt for he knew that the kiss he had pressed on Caprice's lips had been as much a betrayal of Margo as if he had made Caprice his mistress. He had betrayed Cliff too, equally as much. It had not been a kiss given lightly on both sides. There had been a wealth of meaning behind it and he despised his own weakness. He had no doubt confirmed what Caprice had shrewdly always known. He felt that he had been disloyal to Margo in letting Caprice know that he did not love his wife.

Margo—always so gentle and loving and sweet. Considerate for his happiness and well-being and comfort. A splendid wife and the perfect companion. The mother of his two daughters.

Caprice—bewitching and passionate and much too dangerous to his peace of mind. An unhappy woman who snatched at another man's kisses to ease her loneliness.

A wife unfaithful in thought if not in deed and giving as little to her marriage as she got from it. Adam's mother and possessed by her worship of the boy.

Margo—still a lovely woman, as slender and graceful and serene as she had been when he first married her. Those eight years had sped by on wings—a certain indication of their happiness together. He knew that ten years of marriage for Caprice had been at least nine years too much—and her only happiness had been found in Adam. Margo had never failed him in any way and he was grateful for that. He had never once regretted making her his wife.

Before he went to bed that night he knew what he must do. It would be fatal to stay in London with the knowledge that he could see Caprice whenever he wished and know the soaring ecstacy of her kisses. He would return to Mallingham in the morning, return to the safety and peace of Margo's presence, return to sanity and try to forget the madness in his blood which was Caprice.

Even with the need to get home driving him on, he did not forget Serena's birthday present. He drove to Lionel's art gallery and chose a beautiful Degas which depicted a ballet scene. Serena loved to dance and it was apparent that she had a gift for the expression of the joy and love of living that was within her small being. He knew that the painting would give her great pleasure for she had a great love of beauty. He remembered with a quirk of amusement that Francesca had expressed a wish to have a gold watch "like Mummy's" for her birthday a few months previously and now she always wore it on her slender wrist. He knew that she did not value it for its golden, delicate beauty but because it was a replica of Margo's and because it had been an expensive gift.

Serena found beauty in the simplest things—the shape of an oak-leaf, the gleam of sunlight on the lake or the quiet ripple of water when she threw a stone to skim across the surface, the trill of a bird in the trees, the red-gold of her silken hair which she inherited from him, the first uncurling of a rose bud. He was glad of this instinctive appreciation of natural beauty. He found it easy to understand Caprice's obsession with her son for it would be dangerously simple to allow Serena the full possession of his heart, excluding all and everything else.

He knew that Margo was pleased to see him. She came forward as he entered the drawing-room and he knew she had been writing letters at the old carved bureau which was one of the loveliest pieces in the room.

"Luke, we didn't expect you so soon." She took his hands and advanced a smooth cheek for his kiss. He brushed his lips against her skin and then smiled at her.

"I know—but I dislike big cities and I was impatient to get back to Mallingham. It's oppressively warm in London. Where are the girls?"

"Francesca's reading on the lawn. Serena has wandered off somewhere— probably down to the lake."

He felt a spasm of irritation. "I wish you wouldn't let her go down there alone, Margo—she's such a little girl and that lake is very deep."

"Serena is quite intelligent enough to know that she musn't go into the water," she replied calmly. "She likes to be alone —Francesca offered to go with her and she refused her company." She smiled indulgently at her husband. "You worry over Serena quite unnecessarily, my dear."

"Perhaps." He went over to the sideboard and poured himself a drink from the decanter. "Has everything been all right?"

She laughed—a sweet, fluting laugh that held none of the husky richness of Caprice's laugh. "You've only been away three days, darling. Of course everything is all right." She sat down again at the bureau and picked up her fountain pen. "Did you see Daddy's lawyers?"

"Yes—they are going to find out what they can about the London property and let you know. Are you sure you want to sell, Margo?"

"Quite sure." She spoke firmly. "I'm just writing to Lucille. I had a letter from her yesterday—she wants to see me. I thought I'd take the children over to Liscott for a few days next week."

"Why not? It should be rather pleasant."

"You won't want to come with us, I know," she went on. It was apparent that she had everything cut and dried. "You're dining with Richard Hamilton next week

—and then there's the estate accounts to go over with Travis."

"Lord no!" Luke exclaimed. "I can only stand Lucille's husband in small doses." He detested Henry Matthews who called himself a gentleman farmer and knew nothing about the land or its treatment. He could never understand why Lucille had decided to marry the man when she could have chosen a husband out of the many eligible men who flocked about her.

"He is rather a bore," Margo commented. "Why don't you go and find Serena if you're anxious about her, darling?"

He knew her words for the dismissal they were and he grunted. He walked across to the mantelpiece and took down his pipe and tobacco pouch. "Yes, I think I will," he said and left the room by the french windows which opened out on to the stone terrace.

He ran down the steps and walked across the lawn towards Francesca, her golden plaits swinging over her shoulders, her head bowed over an open book. She made a lovely picture with the sunlight glinting on her hair, the serene curve of her cheek resting on her slim hand. She wore a blue dress of some soft material which fell in folds about her on the grass. He felt a thrill of affectionate pride. Serena might be his beloved but he loved this eldest daughter of his. He knew she would grow up to be a cool, serene and lovely woman like her mother with a swift instinct for the right word, the right gesture or the right deed.

"Hallo, Francesca!" he said and he stopped beside her, towering above her.

She looked up from the book. "Oh, hallo, Daddy." She did not seem surprised to see him. Her expression was placidly undisturbed.

He felt in his pocket for the trinket he had brought her—a tiny gold piano with a lid that when lifted caused a pretty Swiss tune to tinkle. He crouched down and put it on top of the book. "I thought you might like this," he said lightly.

She picked it up and looked at it intently, then she lifted the lid and listened to the tune. He knew that she liked it by the slow smile which curved her lips and then she raised shining eyes to his face. "Thank you, Daddy—it's lovely."

"It was very expensive," he teased for he knew from experience that her next question was likely to be: was it expensive?

"I'm sure it was," she returned politely. He ran his hand lightly over her head.

"It's time you had those plaits cut off," he said teasingly for her main vanity was the length and brightness of her hair.

"I shall never cut my hair," she affirmed stoutly.

He pinched her cheek. "We shall see. When you're grown up, it will probably be fashionable to wear your hair short—and lovely ladies always follow the fashion, my pet. What are you reading, Francesca?"

She handed him the book and he read the title: then he riffled through the pages and found that it was composed solely of poetry. He handed the book back to her.

"I like poetry," she said quietly and, he fancied, defensively.

He smiled at her. "So does your mother."

Her eyes lit up again. "Yes, I know."

He straightened up and took his pipe from his pocket. For a long moment he looked down at Francesca and wondered how strange it was that she loved to associate herself with Margo. Did it betray an inner insecurity? Incapability to stand on her own feet? Or merely a sign of her devotion to her mother and a wish to be like her in every way? He could find no fault with this latter suggestion—if Francesca was half as fine a woman as her mother, then some man would be very fortunate one day.

She said quietly, "Serena has gone to the lake, Daddy."

He felt surprise at her percipience. Then he nodded. "So I've been told. I wish you'd gone with her, darling—she's only a little girl and I don't like her to wander around the lake by herself."

"She didn't want me. Serena likes to be alone by the lake—she's quite safe, you know, Daddy," she assured him solemnly.

"I'd better go and make sure," he said and walked on. When he looked back he saw that she had carefully put aside the musical toy and was already immersed in her book of poetry.

He turned and went on down the slope to the woods and then through the pathway to the lake. Children were fascinating little devils. They lived in a world of their own and were inclined to resent the existence of adults or any interference in their private affairs. He thought wryly that many adults never grew out of that private world.

He caught sight of Serena and unconsciously his steps increased their pace. She was barefooted and dancing in and out of the shallows, singing to herself, her red-gold hair loose and flying wildly about her shoulders, her lithe, childlike body expressive and graceful. She sensed his presence before it was possible for her to see him and she stood very still, her head on one side, listening—for all the world like a girl in love waiting for her lover, he thought fleetingly.

Then she ran wildly, madly, across the bumpy hillocks of grass, not caring for the rough sharpness underfoot—and she threw herself into his arms in an ecstacy of joy.

He gathered her close and lifted her into his arms, pressing his cheek against her small, smooth face and grateful for the eager arms about his neck. She was light and sweet-smelling, soft and innocent in her babyhood which he regretted would not last much longer. He felt the wild beating of her passionate heart and the trembling of her eager body.

"Don't go away again, Daddy!" she cried against his neck. "I don't like you to go away."

He kissed her hair. "I have to go away sometimes, darling," he said soothingly. "But I never stay away long, do I? I couldn't leave my baby for long."

"I was lonely," she said tremulously.

He turned her head to look at her sweet and lovely face. "Lonely? But you had Mummy and Francesca."

"I was lonely," she repeated stubbornly. "I'm always lonely wivout you—'cos I love you so much."

Again he held her tight, his heart swelling with love for this innocent baby of his who had learned so young that loneliness comes when the most important person in her life was absent.

"You seemed happy enough just now," he reminded her. "You only dance when you're happy."

"That's 'cos I knew you were home,"

she assured him. "I was misruble—but then something in here," and she touched her little heart with an oddly sincere gesture, "said you'd come home—and I wanted to dance."

He put her down on the ground. Her bare toes were pink and tender: her pale green dress was rumpled and creased and her hair was untidy, a mass of glinting gold in the sunlight.

"I hope you'll always want to dance when I come home," he said oddly and felt a pang for the uncertain future when someone else would take the place of the most important person in her life. But for the present she adored him and there were many years of happiness before them both when each gave the other something that no one else could supply.

He took her hand and they walked back to the lake. He felt a certain pride in her stoicism because even when she trod on a sharp stone or a twig she did not cry out but he felt her small body wince with the pain. He did not offer to carry her for he wanted her to grow up with the capacity to suffer pain courageously. Francesca took after Cliff in that she could not bear physical pain or suffering in others. It was one of those odd twists of Fate which caused Francesca to suffer all the childish ailments when the slightest discomfort caused her acute anguish and yet Serena had never known a day's illness in her young life although she had the capacity for acceptance without protest. She had cut her teeth without any trouble but Francesca's gums had needed lancing before the tiny teeth came through. First attempts at walking and the subsequent falls had brought loud howls from Francesca but no cry from Serena who calmly picked herself up again and toddled on until she fell again when the process was repeated.

He wished his children to be independent so he stood by while Serena struggled with the buttons of her shoes and then, hand in hand, they wandered among the trees and he listened to her eager chatter, grateful for her precocious intelligence and her interest in everything.

That evening, when the children were in bed and he sat with Margo in the cool drawing-room, he looked up from the newspaper and said: "We're lucky to have two nice youngsters. I'm glad they were girls."

She did not take her eyes from the beautiful embroidery she was working. "I've always thought you were a little resentful that I didn't present you with at least one son."

"There's still time," he reminded her with a twinkle in his eyes.

"Oh, I think two's enough," she said. "If you're satisfied with the girls . . ."

"More than satisfied," he said quickly. It was not the first time that Margo had indicated that she was done with child-bearing. He did not blame her. She had had a difficult time with both children. "I'm damn proud of our mutual efforts, darling."

She smiled at that, a swift smile which touched her face with sweetness. "It seems to be hereditary to have girls in my family," she said. "Lucille and I—our two —and her three daughters. We couldn't guarantee a boy the next time."

"Probably not," he agreed. He picked up the box of matches which lay near to his hand and re-lit his pipe. "Francesca's

140

definitely your daughter," he said indistinctly.

"And Serena is yours," she returned. "It worries me a little, Luke—the difference between them. They have so little in common now—I'm afraid they'll drift apart as you and Cliff have done."

"What does it matter? I've never felt the need to see much of Cliff," he replied calmly.

"I think the family bonds should be strengthened, not weakened, as children grow up," she said firmly. "Lucille and I are still very close, you know."

"By the way, I saw Caprice in town yesterday," he said abruptly. He knew he must mention the encounter in case Margo learnt of it accidentally in the future and was disturbed because he had not told her.

She looked up then and her scissors fell from her lap with the swiftness of the movement. "Did you? What was she doing in London?"

"Escaping from Cliff and his friends, I believe," he said as casually as he could. "I had lunch with Lionel and Caprice happened to be in the same restaurant."

He noticed that she visibly relaxed and

wondered why. Then she said: "Oh, you were with Lionel. How is he? Did you ask him when he was coming to see us again?"

She had adroitly changed the subject but he went back to it with deliberate intent. "He sent his love. He looks well—so does Caprice. We talked about the children mostly. She showed me a photograph of Adam—he's getting tall and very handsome." There was a note of envy in his voice which she could not fail to hear.

She bent her head over the embroidery again. "I think you'd like to have a son, Luke."

"Naturally," he said curtly. "Every man would like to have a son. Caprice didn't look a day over twenty-five."

A shadow flitted across her expression then she said serenely: "She can't be much more, I suppose. It's a pity that their marriage isn't more of a success."

He fancied with his senses more acute than usual that there was a note of condemnation for Caprice in her remark. He said defensively: "Don't blame Caprice —Cliff was never cut out for marriage."

"I had not implied that I blamed

Caprice. I imagine that there's fault on both sides."

He rose and went over to her. He bent his head and dropped a kiss on her hair. "Thank goodness we're happily married, darling. You've been absolutely wonderful —no man could wish for a better wife."

She raised a radiant face and he was glad he had given her the few words of praise. "Love is like a delicate plant, darling— and we've carefully tended ours. That's the secret of a happy marriage."

Her remark brought a memory to his mind. His wedding day when Caprice had told him what she considered to be the secret of a happy marriage. Well, he and Margo would not be lovers still after fifty years. They had never been lovers in the sense that Caprice had meant—they had been comfortably fond of each other without the soaring heights and they had known a lot of happiness together.

She took his hand and lifted it briefly to her lips. It was a charming gesture which she frequently did and to him it made up for the lack of passion in her response to his kisses and caresses. It hinted at a love more lasting than passion and he was glad of this. He felt with certainty that many years might pass but he would still know the staunch loyalty and lasting affection of her love.

That night he went into her room and found her sitting up in bed, leaning against the soft pillows, the shaded lamplight illuminating her lovely face. She held a book in her hands which she let fall as he entered. The demure nightgown she wore came up to her throat and the long sleeves fell in ruffles at her wrists. Her golden hair was loose on her shoulders and as he sat down on the bed he twined his fingers in a tress and appreciated the silken texture.

"What are you reading, darling?"

She showed him the open book and he saw immediately that it was poetry. He smiled instinctively. "Why are you amused?" she asked quickly and he sensed that she was hurt by his laughter.

"Because I found Francesca reading the same book this afternoon," he answered. "Your tastes are so similar."

She mused thoughtfully, "I often see myself as a child in Francesca—she's a sweet and unpretentious child."

He repressed the smile that her innocent

words brought, certain that she did not realise the self-praise for the child she had been in her remark.

"She'll never be as sweet or as lovely as her mother," he said warmly and he ran his fingers from her hair across the silk-covered shoulder. His hand tightened and then he leaned forward to kiss her mouth. He noticed as he had noticed so many times that she did not respond with the ardency he had found in her when they were newly married. Her lips were cold and unresponsive and she drew away as soon as she could without offending him. But he was offended and hurt, puzzled by her withdrawal which was all too frequent. If he was not sure that she still loved him as much if not more as always, he would have said that her emotions were cooling towards him. She was affectionate and loving but at the first sign of passion in him she withdrew—it had been thus since before Serena's birth and because he was a considerate husband he had frequently respected her wishes. On those occasions when he spent the night with her, he knew that she was reluctant and he invariably lived with guilt for a few days. It seemed so wrong that he should have to force his wife to accept his lovemaking. Not that he ever actually forced her but he was persistent and she eventually gave in to his caresses and demands.

This was such a night and when she lay sleeping by his side, Luke admitted to himself that he had sought to forget Caprice and that revealing kiss by turning to his wife's embrace. He had hoped to wipe out the guilt in his heart but because he had aroused Margo to ardent response with his own urgency, he felt now that his brief sin against her lay even heavier on him because Margo deserved all his love, all his thoughts and all his loyalty.

8

HE felt at a loss when the big car drove away from Fortune Hall with Margo and the two girls. They were on their way to Liscott, forty miles away, to stay with Lucille and her husband. He was glad they were going for Margo was very fond of her sister. He felt too that the girls should spend more time with their young cousins for there were not many children of their own age in the district. Perhaps that explained why they were so self-sufficient: at least, Francesca was and Serena could be when her father was not constantly with her.

Margo had promised that she would be away no longer than a week, and he knew that she would be anxious about him all the time she was at Liscott. It was amusing really for he was a grown man, capable of finding his own quiet amusements at the Hall and with his friends, and certainly well accustomed to being alone. Francesca had accepted the brief visit to Liscott with the cool placidity she showed to everything but Serena had clung to him in tears until he assured her that it would not be very long, that he would miss her as much as she missed him, and that he would have a surprise for her when she came back. She dried her tears and waited for the departure with a quiet stoicism which barely concealed the anguish in her tiny breast. He felt that it was not good for the child to be so dependent on him, so devoted to him. There was always the risk that one day he would fail her in some way and he knew her sensitive heart could not bear the failure, the fall from the pedestal on which she had placed him.

He had already planned the surprise which would greet her on their return. Drake, his much-loved Labrador, had died two years ago. He had been a good and faithful servant to his master and he was much mourned. Serena indeed had been heartbroken and turned roundly on her then five year old sister when Francesca said coolly that they could always get another dog. She had declared passionately that she would never want another dog, that she wanted Drake. She had wept copiously when Luke had solemnly and with pain in his own heart presided over the dog's funeral in a corner of the woods he had loved so much and erected a stone memorial to his faithful companion. Now, two years later, he felt that Serena would understand and accept a replacement and he had arranged for the delivery of two small Labrador puppies, one for each of his daughters. They would learn to care for their dogs and how to train them to be obedient and well-behaved. The training would also have its own effect on the girls, he hoped. They were both obedient to a certain extent: then if a request—never an order—clashed with Francesca's own wishes she would quietly and calmly point out that she could not comply and give logical and reasonable explanations for her disobedience; Serena, on the other hand, was illogical and wilful and preferred to follow the dictates of her own personality at times.

As he entered the house, he thought ruefully that he had never realised how much psychology had to be applied in the upbringing of children. It was useless to treat them all alike. They were individuals in their own right and he preferred them to have minds of their own. He knew little of Adam but he felt vaguely that the boy was spoilt by Caprice and snubbed by Cliff —yet he also felt that neither treatment would harm the boy in any way. Recalling that proud and natural arrogance reflected in his photograph, the good breeding which was evident in him, the dark and intelligent eyes, the sensitive mouth and the independent stance, he was sure that nothing would make or break Adam but his own will and he would prove to be a worthy heir to the Fortune birthright.

The house seemed strangely empty and he decided to walk off the feeling of despondency which had settled on his spirits. He trudged down the drive and through the gates and set his direction for the big, rambling old house where his friend Richard Hamilton lived. He liked and respected Richard: they had many a friendly argument on various subjects; they usually ended their evenings together with a game of chess and it was a great feather in Luke's cap if he managed to beat his skilful friend. He was a bachelor but this did not imply a dislike for women.

He enjoyed feminine company but he was strictly a celibate. He admired Margo and spoke of her with warm praise: he was fond of children and understood them— he never made the mistake of talking down to them in a patronising manner and Francesca and Serena appreciated this; he had a great affection for Luke and this was returned in full measure.

Finding that Luke was alone, Richard pressed him to stay for dinner and he made no protest. It was very late when he finally left the old house and set out on foot for the Hall. Richard had offered him his car but he had refused, assuring his friend that the night air would clear his head which ached a little from the fumes of tobacco and the excellent brandy he had consumed.

He walked through the quiet lanes to the gates of the Hall. It was a warm and peaceful night. The heavy scent of flowers from the gardens reached his nostrils. The last goodnights were trilled from the birds in the trees. Darkness shrouded the old Hall and the grounds and the very atmosphere was somnolent.

He heard the rustle of a dress and he

paused in his tracks, looking about him, bewildered. At first he saw nothing, then a few yards away from him he caught sight of the faint gleam of a light gown and the same moment he heard a husky whisper: "Luke!" It was Caprice and now he realised that he had sensed it all along.

He moved towards her and she came towards him. They met and he looked down at her. In the dim shadows, he could see the gleam of her eyes and the flash of white teeth as she laughed up at him gleefully.

"What the devil are you doing here?" he asked, trying to sound firm and exasperated but only succeeding in sounding delighted.

She raised herself on her toes to brush his lips fleetingly with her mouth. "It's a long story, Luke," she said. "I thought you were never coming—I've been waiting ages. Vernon said you were probably with Mr. Hamilton—whoever he might be—were you?"

"Richard Hamilton—he's a friend of mine. Yes. We've been playing chess."

She linked her hand in his arm and they turned to walk across the lawns towards the terrace which was palely illuminated by the lights from the house.

"And I've been playing patience all evening—I didn't know I could be so patient." She laughed again, a soft chuckle which stirred his blood.

Unexpected as her presence was—and no doubt he would later be angry about it—he was thrilled to know that once again she walked by his side and linked her hand in his arm. Explanations could come later. For the moment he would cherish her nearness and enjoy the surge of his blood and the pounding of his heart.

"Luke—why did you slip away like that?" she asked huskily. "Running away again?"

"Yes, I suppose so." There was no point in denial. No doubt she knew well enough why he had left London so precipitately.

"You're so different to other men," she sighed. "Not many men would have run away from me, Luke."

"I was afraid of what might happen between us," he said frankly. "We're not children, Caprice—and when I kissed you, I think you realised how little it would take for me to betray Margo, Cliff and myself."

"Remembering your duty again?" she mocked lightly. Then she was suddenly sober. "Yes, I understood why you went. I had already decided to leave London myself the following morning—I telephoned your hotel to tell you so and learned that you had settled your account and returned to Mallingham."

He stopped short and tried to see her expression in the shadow. "You were leaving? Why?"

"Dear Luke." Her voice was warm and tender. "You really don't know, do you?"

"No."

"Because we're not children, Luke." She gave him back his own words. "I've never yet flouted my marriage vows. I'm older now—I've learnt not to snatch at happiness, my dear. I believe it will come in time if I'm entitled to it—I've no wish to throw away my chance of it by indulging in a light affair with you."

Her words hurt him beyond expression. It would have been nothing more than a light affair to her—while he lived constantly with an all-consuming love which never gave him peace.

She walked on and up the stone steps. They entered the drawing-room and still he was silent. Now the light fell full on them both and she could see the grim line of his mouth and the stark pain in his eyes. He saw that she wore a flowing dress of ice-blue satin and he closed his mind against the memory of the first time he had seen her in a box at the theatre, wearing a dress of identical colour and looking as beautiful then as now. The years seemed to leave no mark on her creamy skin or on that slim and graceful body. She would be beautiful when she was an old woman for her beauty was in the grace of her movements, the classical line of bone formation and the expressiveness of her dark eyes. He felt that they would forever glow and kindle with that burning vitality.

She said swiftly: "Darling, I've hurt you —forgive me."

She had never used this endearment to him and it struck him forcibly that it was an impulsive atonement for her words. How generous she was with that swift and sincere apology. He could not continue to be distressed by her casual remark.

He smiled down at her. "Tell me how you got here, Caprice—and why you came."

She threw herself into a deep armchair and curled her feet under her. "It probably seems most mysterious but the explanation is simple. I told you I was going home to Veerham at the weekend. Well, I changed my mind. Cliff rang up to say his friends were staying another week and I couldn't face that impossible crowd. I had more or less exhausted my sources of amusement and entertainment in London. Then I happened to meet Lucille Matthews in Oxford Street—Margo's sister. I've met her off and on throughout the years through mutual friends. In casual conversation, she told me that Margo was going to stay with her this week at Liscott and that she was looking forward to seeing Francesca and Serena again. So Caprice told herself that Luke would be alone and, possibly, lonely—I decided to spend a few days with you and here I am." She said this last so simply that Luke laughed.

"I shall never understand you," he said

lightly. "Last week you were all for running away from me and temptation—today you come blindly forward to meet it."

"I know I'm illogical," she said. "But I felt that I'd earned a few days of happiness with you, Luke—we've had such little time together in all these years. I want to know all the everyday things about you. I want to know your companionship and your laughter. I want to share your days with you."

He sat down heavily in an opposite chair. "I should have thought you'd want to rush back to Veerham to be with Adam."

"I adore Adam—I don't need to tell you that. A part of me is missing when I'm not with him. But there are times when a woman needs the company and the attentions of a man—when her child, dear though he is, just isn't enough. One day Adam won't need me any more." She said this bravely but he knew the thought caused her pain. "I like to think that I shall still be attractive to men then—I mustn't get rusty, my dear." Her rich laugh rang out. "So I thought I'd practice my charms on you for a few days."

She was so blatant that he could not help smiling across at her. There was something so childlike about her on occasions as though she said whatever outrageous or fanciful thing might be running through her mind at that moment. She reminded him vividly of Serena as she sat with her stockinged feet curled under her, high-heeled shoes kicked on to the carpet, the ice-blue dress falling in folds about her. There was a suggestion of the same wayward wilfulness, the impulsive warmth, the need to love and be loved.

"I suppose you know that you place me in a damned awkward situation."

She was deliberately obtuse, raising her eyebrows innocently. "My dear Luke, surely no one could object to Lady Veerham visiting her brother-in-law for a few days?"

"That isn't what I meant," he said sharply.

Her voice softened. "No, I know, Luke. I'm quite mad—but I intend to enjoy this temporary madness. Call it spring fever, if you like." She smiled slowly across at him, a seductive smile. "I'll leave in the morning if you want me to go, Luke—but I don't think you do."

"No, I don't—damn you!" The words came harshly. He rose swiftly and strode over to her. With fierce passion which held more than a little anger in it, he caught her face between his hands and kissed her full on her lips. It was a long and urgent kiss—then he let his caress wander from the curve of her mouth to her cheek, her eyes, her hair, the lobe of her small ear and then tracing gently to her neck and from thence to the curve of her breast above the low line of her gown.

She put her hands up against his chest as he would have drawn her ever closer and pushed him away. "No." The word was forced from her and as he slowly straightened up he saw that her breast heaved with emotion and that tears glistened in her eyes. He did not doubt that he had kindled passion in the depths of her being but he was innately thankful that she had thrown that negative word at him. It brought him quickly to his senses and he realised how near he had been to betraying Margo in her own home.

Caprice stood up and slipped her feet into the flimsy shoes. Then she walked to the window and stared out into the darkness.

He came up behind her and put his hands on her shoulders. Gently he drew her close and she relaxed against him as though conscious that she now had nothing to fear from his passion. She was trembling and the light caught the streaks of tears on her cheeks."

She said quietly: "If I stay, Luke, you must promise not to kiss me again—like that."

He caught his breath. One taste of ecstasy—and she denied him more. But he knew that it was a wise request and he knew that he would comply with it. They would be deliberately laying themselves open to temptation otherwise—and he could never live with himself or with Margo again if he possessed Caprice. His passion had cooled now and he was tender as he touched her hair with his lips. "I promise, Caprice. I'm sorry, my dear."

"More apologies," she said mockingly. "A man thinks he has only to apologise and a woman forgets."

He stiffened and anger swept through him. "If there is one trait I dislike in you, it's your frequent generalisations about men," he said coldly.

She turned to face him and slipped her arms about him. It was an instinctive gesture and one that held nothing of passion. "I base my rather cynical knowledge on one man only," she said gently. "But I should always remember that you're different to Cliff."

He held her close for a brief moment then he let her go and walked over to the sideboard. He felt that he deserved a drink and carefully, trying to control the shaking of his hands, he poured whisky into a glass. He said over his shoulder: "Sherry, Caprice?"

She laughed huskily. "Make it whisky, please."

He was a little startled but he complied. She came over and took the glass from his hand. She raised the glass and mocked him with her eyes. "Here's to our self control!" She moved away and sat down again in the deep armchair, legs stretched in front of her, one hand resting lightly on the arm. She said wearily: "Is it worth denying

161

myself the happiness you could give me, Luke? I think of Cliff and his frequent associations with other women—and then I know it is worth it because I will not sink to his level!"

He stood very still, looking at the liquor in his glass, swirling it gently so that it caught the light. "Why don't you and Cliff separate? Why do you cling to a marriage that's been on the rocks for years?"

She shrugged. "You mean divorce? If I gave him grounds, he would divorce me—but he would take Adam. The courts would give Adam into his custody because I had proved myself to be an unfit person to have him. That I will not risk."

"You could divorce him," he suggested. "From what you say, you have grounds in plenty."

"Marriage doesn't bind Cliff very much—he lives his own life and pleases no man but himself. He's as free now as he ever was. I'm content with things as they are. My freedom wouldn't bring me any happiness."

"You could marry again. Someone who would make you happy."

She looked at him with an enigmatic

gleam in her dark eyes. "I happen to know a man who would make me happy—but marriage is out of the question."

"He's married already?" He asked the question while his heart was seized in an agonising grip of pain. So there was another man—and he had been fool enough to read more into her response to his kisses than actually existed. She was a neglected wife and a passionate woman. He could not blame her for seeking to prove that she was still capable of rousing a man to passion.

"That, of course. Other reasons." She drained the fiery whisky. "No, Luke—let's leave things as they are. As long as I have Adam, I can put up with Cliff for a husband." She sighed briefly. "You're happy, aren't you? With Margo, I mean. I envy you so much."

He moved across and sat down in the armchair he had previously occupied. He regarded her steadily. "Yes, I'm very happy. Your prophecies didn't come about, Caprice. You told me that Margo would bore me to death—you were wrong. You said that she was a cold woman—you were wrong again. I think we have the ideal marriage—it's proving very successful, anyway, and we have two delightful daughters to strengthen our love for each other." He spoke firmly for he did not want her to think that his kisses had implied anything but a momentary attraction for a beautiful woman. She could assume what she liked about his feelings for her but he meant to disprove these assumptions. As their eyes met, he felt that she saw through all he had said and her gaze seemed to plumb his innermost emotions. It was futile to pretend to Caprice. She was far too percipient to believe his firm assurance that no other woman meant anything in his life—and she knew instinctively that she was the other woman. He dropped his gaze, feeling uncomfortably easy to see through.

She said mockingly: "If Margo knew you as well as I do, you'd never get away with it, Luke. But she's the type of woman who sees only what she wants to see—she's conveniently blind to the truth." She added unexpectedly: "I hope so—because I happen to like her and I wouldn't want her to be hurt in any way."

"Margo is quite capable of facing facts

—unpleasant or otherwise," he said defensively.

"Then she knows? In that case, she's a very wise woman. I would expect her to be jealous and determined to keep you out of my way. But no doubt she trusts you completely—and I'm sure you'd never let her down in any way."

He gestured swiftly. "Look here, Caprice—what are you trying to say?"

She smiled. "You think I'm trying to force you into an admission? That's unnecessary, Luke. You're in love with me and I've known it for years. If I hadn't been married to Cliff, you would never have married Margo—I've always understood your motives, my dear."

Words of protest flew to his lips and then remained stillborn. She would only laugh at him with those lovely eyes if he denied the charge. He said flatly: "So you know. I won't deny it, Caprice. I do love you—I shall always love you." He had never believed that the words would be spoken. But it was out in the open now, mentioned frankly and without embarrassment or shame.

Her expression was very tender. "Luke,

the best thing that has happened in my life—apart from Adam—is knowing that a man like you is in love with me. I think it's the only thing that's kept me sane all these years while I've known absolute hell with your brother."

Her words absolved him from the guilt which had always lived with him since his first realisation that he loved her. He leaned forward. "If that is the truth, Caprice—then I'm glad of my love for you. I've tried to fight it, to ignore it—certainly I've done my best to conceal it."

"You were fighting a losing battle from the start," she said gently.

"In more ways than one," he sighed. "You know as well as I do that nothing can come of it. I'm glad you know, Caprice. It's been difficult not to tell you a thousand times during the last eight years. But it's a love that can never know fulfilment and I accepted that long ago. I'm married to Margo—and I am happily married, my dear—you can understand that?"

She nodded. "Yes, of course. I told you many years ago that you have the capacity to accept the inevitable and make the best of what life offers you. The Hall instead of Veerham—Margo instead of me—I admire you for that, Luke."

"This man—you're in love with him? The one you mentioned." He spoke stiffly. It was futile to hope that she could care for him—futile because it was unlikely and because even if she did return his love, their lives remained still as incomplete. If they both obtained their freedoms, he could never marry his brother's ex-wife while Cliff lived.

She nodded. "With all my heart. Without him—and the knowledge that he loves me too—I think I should die, Luke." She spoke simply. "He means more to me than Adam even—because I've made myself accept the fact that one day Adam will not need me any more. But I think I shall always need the man I love as much as he needs me—even if we cannot be together." She rose abruptly and walked across the room to place her empty glass on the sideboard. "It's getting late, Luke—you'll forgive me if I go to bed?"

He nodded and rose too. "I'm going up myself." He followed her from the room and they walked together up the wide staircase, her hand lightly on his arm. At the top of the stairs, she turned to him. She held her fingertips briefly to her lips and then placed them gently against his lips.

"Dear Luke," she murmured. "At least I can talk to you and know you will understand."

"I try to understand," he said quietly. "But I sometimes wonder what will be the end of it all for us both."

"Only the passing years will prove what is in store for us, Luke," she said gently and then she went into her bedroom. The door closed quietly behind her and for a long moment he stood staring at the wooden panels, envious of her quiet faith and acceptance. Who would have believed that she possessed such a fund of patience? He had not realised her depth of quiet courage which enabled her to accept the lonely emptiness of her life because she firmly believed that one day she would know ultimate happiness.

9

CAPRICE stayed at Fortune Hall for five days. They were very happy together. No further mention was made of their emotions and Luke kept strictly to his promise. He made no attempt to kiss her. Their only contacts were when she linked her hand in his arm as they walked about the grounds and when, each night before she closed her bedroom door, she fleetingly touched her fingertips first to her own lips and then to his, with her eyes glowing warmly into his.

Luke recalled the thrill of pride he had known all those years ago when she had promised to persuade Cliff to bring her to the Hall and he had anticipated showing her the lovely old house and the pleasant charms of the estate. Well, she and Cliff had never stayed together at the Hall. Their few visits had been brief indeed. When Caprice had stayed overnight at the Hall on that one occasion before he married Margo, she had seen little of the grounds or the house.

Now he could show her over his home for they had time and to spare at their disposal. He was glad that she did not profess to prefer Fortune Hall to Veerham —as Margo had done. Quite possibly Margo had been sincere—but he sometimes wondered if she had not dutifully tried to ease his longing for Veerham which never altered as the years passed.

Caprice would never pretend to something she did not feel. She was essentially honest and outspoken and although he found her frankness disconcerting at times, he also admired it. She said that Veerham was the more beautiful of the two estates but Fortune Hall was easier to live up to—and he knew instinctively what she meant. Veerham demanded dignity and grandeur and arrogance. The Hall was a place where one could be perfectly at ease. Caprice put it in a nutshell when she said lightly that Veerham was the family seat: Fortune Hall was a very lovely home.

They found many subjects for conversation. She was intelligent and quick-witted, observant and percipient. She had a lively sense of humour and her laughter rang out frequently during those few days. They were like two children as they wandered hand in hand through the woods or swam together in the lake. The years seemed to fall away from them and they forgot everything but the enjoyment of each other. Only at nights, when Luke lay restless in his bed, too conscious that Caprice lay sleeping in a room on the other side of the corridor, did his thoughts turn to Margo with a brief regret that they had never known this keen delight in each other's company, this eager anticipation of every new day and the reluctance to part for a few hours of the night. Regret but never guilt for he knew that he had not taken anything away from Margo. She had never had his heart wholly and utterly as Caprice had. His great affection for her was untouched and inviolate. He knew that he could welcome her home when she returned from Liscott with a clear conscience and peace of mind and a certain pleasure in her return.

Caprice threw herself into the enjoyment of her brief happiness with Luke and every day he found fresh cause to love her. She was glowing with life and vitality and energy. She was a graceful and excellent swimmer and Luke found that she left him way behind as she streaked across the lake with a powerful, lithe stroke. It was early days for swimming but she took no notice of the coolness of the water and seemed to find it invigorating. Certainly her slim body responded to the exercise and the swift towel-rubbing she gave it afterwards. Every muscle, every nerve seemed to be toned to its full extent. She could walk for miles with Luke by her side and she never tired. She seemed to shed some of her sophistication and elegance and he found her most appealing when she loosened her dark hair and let it be whipped by the breeze. She wore crimson slacks and sweater for the most part because then it did not matter what they did or where they went, she assured him lightly. If her sandals hurt her feet, she slipped them off and walked barefoot beside him, revelling in the freedom from convention and restraint. She seemed young, really young, and the years slipped from his shoulders— they walked and talked, laughed and sang, swam and rode and fished for minnows in the lake. In the evenings, when she had changed into one of her many lovely gowns—it surprised him to find how many clothes she had brought with her for the brief stay—she would sit at the piano in the drawing-room and play to him while he drew a chair up to the blazing fire in the hearth, his pipe in his hand, a drink on the table beside him and contentment stealing over him. It pleased him to fancy that he and Caprice were married—he rested his head on the back of the chair and closed his eyes and visualised what life would be if it were the truth. It would surely always be as wonderful as this— even if she could not love him as he loved her. He was sure that she was very fond of him and he knew that she found him physically attractive. Wryly, he told himself that no one would believe in their strict self-control—certainly Margo, if she could see them occasionally, swimming in the lake or walking hand in hand through the woods or laughing together over a childish joke, would be convinced that they were lovers. But they never had been in the complete sense of the word and it was most unlikely that they ever would be.

When she left the piano, she would come and sit on a low stool by his chair and with his hand lightly toying with her dark curls, her expression vivacious and beautiful, they would talk beside the fire until the early hours.

Yes, he could imagine Caprice to be his wife—until that moment when they paused outside her bedroom door and she lightly bestowed a proxy kiss on his lips. Then she went into her room and closed the door quietly but firmly—and he had to fight down the desire which flooded him and go to his lonely bed.

At last it was time for her to leave. Margo had telephoned to assure Luke that she would be coming back with the children on the following day and asked anxiously if all was well with him. He knew then that he should casually introduce the subject of Caprice and tell his wife of her visit to the Hall. But the words died on his lips and he lacked the courage to speak the truth. Instead he said that he had been fine, that he missed her and the girls, and that he would drive over to Liscott himself to bring them home. He knew she was pleased by the sudden

174

warmth in her voice. Then she rang off and for a long moment he looked at the receiver in his hand.

Caprice was standing by the door, listening to his side of the conversation. Now she moved to his side and put her arms about him. He turned and drew her close, with a movement that was almost convulsive in its longing.

They were silent, each seeking some silent comfort from the other. Then Caprice said softly: "So this is the end, Luke. I'd better leave today."

He tilted her chin and looked deep into her eyes. "It's been wonderful, my darling. Thank you for these few precious days."

She sighed. "It's been wonderful for me, too." She drew away from him abruptly. "I must pack—I daren't put off going, Luke. It's going to be hard enough —so I must do it as quickly as possible. You understand?"

"Yes, I understand."

He watched her swift departure and then he put a hand through his hair in a despairing gesture. The pain in his heart swelled until it burst its bounds and shuddered violently through his entire body. He felt that he had never known such agony and knew that the poets who called the parting of lovers a little death spoke truly. He felt as though he had received a death-blow and he swayed on his feet while blackness engulfed him for a brief second. It was with an effort that he pulled himself together and walked across to the bell-push to summon Vernon.

When the man arrived, he ordered coffee to be brought to the drawing-room immediately. Vernon looked at him anxiously before he turned to leave the room. "Are you all right, sir? A drop of brandy? You look very pale, sir."

"I'm all right," Luke snapped and then added more pleasantly: "Just a bad head-ache, Vernon. Lady Veerham will be leaving soon—would you have her car brought to the door?"

He wondered idly as the man went out if the servants knew of the situation between him and Caprice. What they didn't know was probably supplied by conjecture, he thought wryly. As long as they didn't gossip in front of Margo or the children, he didn't care. His conscience was clear and he could look Margo in the eyes with the full knowledge of that fact.

Caprice came slowly into the room and she had changed into an exquisitely-tailored suit. Her dark hair was bound tightly against her head. She was very pale and her eyes were very sombre. They had lost their vital glow.

He went to her immediately and took her hands. "Caprice—darling!" he said urgently. "I'm beginning to wonder how I'm going to live without you!"

She forced a smile to her lips. "Life goes on, my dear." She hesitated briefly. "I'm glad we weren't . . . foolish, Luke. Happiness is never lasting when it's taken at someone else's expense, you know."

"I know that—but I can't help feeling that we've wasted these precious days, Caprice," he said urgently.

Her eyes reproached him. "Wasted them? But we've been so happy together —and you've proved to me that a man can truly love a woman without insisting that they go to bed together. I appreciate that, Luke."

"You're right," he said humbly. "I shouldn't have said that. Of course they haven't been wasted—but I do feel that to own you completely—if only once—would enable me to face the future without protest."

She shook her head. "It's better this way, my dear. You would never be satisfied with making love to me once—be honest with yourself."

Vernon entered the room with the tray and they broke apart, their hands swiftly unlinked. Without any change of expression, the man placed the tray on a low table and withdrew from the room.

Caprice sat down by the table and began to pour the coffee. Luke noticed that her hands were calm and even, her gestures deft and graceful and unfaltering. He found it in his heart to wish that she was not calm; that their parting meant as much to her as it did to him.

She handed him his coffee and then picked up her own cup and stirred it thoughtfully. "Luke—when we were talking the other night and I told you about the man I loved—you didn't know to whom I referred, did you?"

He looked surprised by the sudden question. "No. Do I know him then?"

Her lips quirked with brief amusement. "Very well. Better than anyone else—except me."

He wrinkled his brow. "I'm damned if I know . . ."

"Luke! Luke! Don't be so blind," she cried. "You're the man I love. I've loved you since the first day I met you at Veerham. I never forgot you after our meeting at the theatre—but I fell in love with you when I went to Veerham with Cliff and you were so obviously unhappy about leaving your home and so appealingly pompous to cover it up."

He slammed his coffee cup down on the tray, uncaring that it spilt slightly. "Me?" he exclaimed. "Caprice—if you dare to tease me . . ." He could not go on for he was choked with emotion.

She placed her cup carefully on the table. She held out her hand to him. "Come here—come and sit by me, Luke." He rose like a man spellbound and did as she asked. She clasped his hand in both of her slim cool hands and raised it to her cheek with a child-like, loving gesture. "Dear Luke," she murmured and then he knew that she did not tease. That she had in fact always loved him and had told him openly every time she used that familiar endearment—but he had been blind to the tenderness of the glowing eyes and deaf to the gentle adoration in her voice. With a sigh that was almost a groan, he caught her against him and buried his face in her dark hair. Gently she caressed the nape of his neck and the crisp, thick hair which seemed to cling to her fingers as though bewitched by her touch. Her slim body melted against his and the love which flowed between them eased a little of the pain in his heart.

"You let me think it was someone else—these last few days when it would have been the crowning joy to know that you loved me as I love you," he accused with reproach in his voice, raising his head to look into her eyes. "Caprice—you must have known you would hurt me. Why the devil did you conceal your real feelings?"

Now she cupped his face in her hands and her eyes were full of love for him. Her cool lips brushed his and then she said softly: "Because we would definitely have been . . . foolish if I had admitted my love for you. Would you have taken no for an answer then, Luke? Could you have kept your promise? Wouldn't you have insisted that we take our happiness while we could? Be truthful, my darling." Again that fleeting touch of her mouth against his.

He closed his eyes against the pain and the ecstasy which was almost pain in itself. "Yes," he sighed. "Yes, we'd have known real happiness if you had told me this when you arrived the other night."

"We have known real happiness, Luke," she reminded him gently. "Now, let us be sensible. You and I both know that we were made for each other, Luke. I should never have married Cliff—and you should never have married Margo. But we cannot plan our destinies—and we have to face facts. The foremost fact is that we can never be together—I was mad to come here this week and I only hope that no one ever attaches the wrong significance to my stay. We must cherish the memory of our few days together, my darling—and in future see as little of each other as ever and when we meet—well, I shall probably never reveal the Caprice that you've known while I've been here and you will be my courteous and utterly charming brother-in-law."

He struggled for composure. "You sound so matter of fact," he said bitterly. "You've made up your mind that there is no future for us. Be sensible, you say—there's no sense in our love for one another."

She chided him gently. "Darling, this isn't a sudden and swift attachment. We've loved each other for years—and we've managed to find contentment in our separate lives. So we will again."

He shook his head stubbornly. "Now that I've known what a wonderful person you are—how happy you can make me—I'll never be content again."

She placed her fingers over his lips quickly. "Do you want me to regret that I came?"

He looked deep into her eyes and knew that she was completely honest. If he did not resume the threads of his life with Margo and know the familiar ease and contentment of married life again, then she would always regret her visit to the Hall, always regret that she had stirred yearning in him for a richer happiness, always regret that she had created a rift between him and Margo.

"You must never regret that," he said fervently. "It's been wonderful, Caprice—a happiness I never thought to know."

She smiled warmly, tenderly. "Yes, my darling, it has been wonderful." She glanced at her watch. "I'm going now, Luke." She rose swiftly to her feet and began to pull on her gloves. "Now I am eager to get home to Adam—you eased the longing for him, my dear, but now it's as strong as ever." She looked down at him and then swiftly bent to press her lips on his hair. "I'm leaving a part of me with you—take good care of my heart, my dearest."

He scanned her face with eagerness, anguish within him, searching for some sign of weakness, of reluctance. But she was composed and very sure of herself. "You can walk out just like that," he said, snapping his fingers.

She nodded but her eyes were tender. "I have to. Believe me, I could stay with you as easily as that." And she too snapped her fingers. "But we can't just think of ourselves, Luke. There's Margo and your two daughters—my son Adam. I couldn't involve him in any scandal—and you know in your heart that you'd never forgive yourself if you hurt Margo or tainted the lives of Francesca and Serena."

"I know there's only one thing to do," he said dully. "But it seems very hard at the moment. I love you so much, Caprice —we belong together and I am incomplete without you."

Her eyes suddenly glistened with bright tears. "Your love will help me to go on without you—and I want you always to remember that I love you. It's twice as hard for me, you know—I haven't someone as kind and good and understanding as Margo in the background."

He was filled with contrition. He rose and took her in his arms. "I'm sorry, my dearest. I was thinking only of myself— pure selfishness."

She fought back the tears. Tears of pain, of futility, of longing and bitterness. "I only ask one thing from you, Luke—go on loving me. I'm not taking anything from Margo because she's content with your affection—and she's never known your love in the way that I have."

"I shall always love you," he said very quietly and the kiss he laid gently on her mouth sealed his words.

He thought the pain would never lessen. The big house was empty and desolate. He found no comfort in the familiar beauty of the woods and the lake—for the memory of Caprice walked beside him and he was tormented with the need for her.

Yet as Margo held out her hands to him and offered her cheek for his kiss, he felt a strange balm steal over him, a comforting warmth, which increased as Francesca kissed him fleetingly and Serena flung her small arms around his neck and bestowed passionate kisses on his face and neck. The anguish of the lover left him at that moment and the quiet content of being both husband and father took over in his soul.

On the way home, Serena insisted on sitting in the front with him and the journey passed quickly while he listened avidly to her childish prattle and the affectionate assurances that although she had enjoyed the stay at Liscott she had missed him very much. Margo and Francesca sat in the back and occasionally his wife shushed the small child in front and imparted family news and gossip to Luke.

He could never understand why Margo did not discover that Caprice had stayed at the Hall for those five days. It seemed that the servants had joined in a conspiracy not to let drop a hint in casual conversation. He had seen nothing more of Richard while Caprice was at the Hall. Not wanting interruptions of any kind, he had told Vernon not to admit any callers to the house and they had been left entirely on their own to follow pleasures and pursuits in privacy. He had excused himself from a dinner party and a bridge engagement, seeking to keep all his time for that brief interlude with the woman he loved. Margo did not express any curiosity as to his activities while she was away and he offered no explanation. They settled down to their usual affectionate companionship and he occupied himself with the affairs which should have known his attention during that week.

Weeks later, he heard through a mutual friend that Caprice had taken Adam to the South of France to join Cliff who was staying with friends and he saw nothing of her for many weary months of heartache and longing. But he found his comfort in the knowledge that she had always loved him and that nothing could ever come between their secret love for each other.

He could not find it in his heart to be guilty for he gave Margo the loyal affection she had always known and she did not suffer because his heart belonged to Caprice and his thoughts were constantly with her.

There was a very anxious period when even the thought of Caprice was driven out of his mind. For Margo gave him a son almost at the cost of her own life—and it was then that he learned the reason for her cool withdrawal from him since Serena's birth, her apparent reluctance to know his passion.

It was a difficult birth and Luke sensed the anxiety in Heath who attended her. The girls had been sent to Liscott and he was glad that their childish happiness could not be tinged with the gloom and despondency which was prevalent at the Hall.

Luke cornered Heath when he came

down from Margo's room, looking strained and weary.

"How is my wife?" he demanded anxiously.

Heath shook his head. "She's very tired —and there's nothing I can do for her." He looked sternly at Luke. "It was very foolish for her to undertake another pregnancy. I made it very clear to her when Serena was born that the next time could be fatal."

Luke stared at him in dismay. "I knew nothing of that," he said. "Why didn't Margo tell me?"

Heath shrugged. "How should I know? Surely she didn't keep you in absolute ignorance of the fact?"

Luke's lips tightened into a grim line. "I'm sorry that you should doubt me, Heath—but Margo has never said anything to me about it. You don't imagine I'm the kind of man to insist on my wife having children when it could be dangerous?"

Heath apologised. He was tired and anxious, he explained. Luke offered him a drink and the elderly doctor accepted it thankfully.

"She's going to be all right, though?" Luke asked with fear pulsing in his veins.

"I hope so. It's a tricky business—having children." He sighed. "I wanted her to have this child at Mallingham Hospital but she was stubborn. She said that she knew it was going to be a boy and that you would want him to be born at the Hall." He looked at Luke from beneath bushy eyebrows. "I gather a son was rather a necessity—for the sake of the entail?"

"Of course not!" Luke snapped. "I have two daughters—that would have been sufficient. But Margo seemed to have the idea that my heart was set on a son—I admit I've been pleased at the prospect. Every man wants a son, after all. But not at the risk of his wife's life." He drained his glass. He had needed the drink as much as Heath.

"I shall do my best, of course," Heath said quietly. "But I thought you should be prepared for the worst—just in case." He turned to leave the room then at the door he paused and looked back. "Just for the record—if it's a question of your wife or the child?"

189

"My wife, of course!" Luke said without hesitation and there was anger in his voice that this silly old fool should have imagined there was any question of his answer.

Heath nodded. "Very well."

Left alone, Luke had another drink and then threw himself into an armchair, covering his eyes with his hand. Why hadn't Margo told him the truth? Now, all too clearly, he realised why she had been so cold since Serena was born. In her heart must always have been the fear of another child and perhaps her own death. He found himself praying fervently that she would be all right—and the child too if it were possible, for Margo had been happy with the thought of giving him a son. Not once during these last months had she shown any sign of fear about the ordeal before her. He had never had reason to believe that she didn't want to have this child. How courageous she was. How fine and good—and what a marvellous actress to cover up her innermost emotions so successfully. He wondered how little he really knew his own wife. They had never been close in the sense of knowing how the other's mind worked or how the other's emotions were touched. Despite their happiness in their marriage, they had always lived separate lives, found their own interests, developed their own friendships. Not even the girls had brought them any closer although they both loved their daughters—he with a passionate intensity, Margo with a quiet, unswerving and loyal love which made itself felt just as strongly.

It seemed an eternity before Heath returned to him and this time there was a lightness to his step which presaged that all was well. Luke leaped from his chair and searched his face anxiously.

Heath smiled. "Well, you have a son—fine and healthy—and over eight pounds. You owe it all to your wife's stamina and courage."

"She's all right?" The words were little more than a whisper.

"She's come through it very well. In a moment, you may see her—but only for a moment or two. Then she must rest—it will be a few weeks before she's up and about but you must be thankful that she can look forward to being up and about."

Margo had accepted his almost

incoherent pleas of forgiveness for his lack of understanding with a tired smile and a warm, tender touch of her hand on his cheek. She knew now that there could never be another child—but Luke was content. He had his wife—and he had a son, a child both handsome and healthy. They named him Michael.

10

CLIFF came to Michael's christening. He came alone for Adam had recently been very ill and Caprice had taken him abroad for a spell of convalescence.

He seemed to be ageing suddenly and Luke realised that his brother was forty years old. His body had thickened. He seemed to have shed some of his old gaiety and recklessness.

The night before the christening, he sat with Luke in the library, a brandy glass in his hand, toying with a cigarette between the fingers of the other hand. Luke was trying to be hospitable to his brother: trying to forget the many years of unhappiness he had caused Caprice; trying to stem the flood of jealousy because this man was not only his brother but the husband of the woman he loved, and the dislike which filled him as he studied those sensual lips, the dissolute lines about the eyes, the heaviness of the jaw, the restlessness which had always been one of his traits.

Cliff was silent for a long time but Luke was busy with his own thoughts so he did not mind. The two men sat opposite each other—brothers, linked by blood but not by affection.

Suddenly Cliff said: "God, I'm tired. Tired of the eternal chase after life and excitement. I suppose I'm getting old— but I feel that my life has been pretty empty, you know, Luke."

His brother made no reply. What could he answer? Only that it was Cliff's own fault if he found life empty. That he had no need to chase after life and excitement —he could find plenty on his own door- step if he chose to appreciate it.

Cliff went on: "Oh, I know you think I'm a fool. There's never been much love lost between us, Luke—I'm not worried about that. We're made on different lines, that's all. But I envy you."

Now Luke said, startled: "Envy me?" While he was filled with envy for his brother's possession of Caprice, his fine son, Veerham—all the things that Luke would have liked to own.

Cliff looked up with a trace of a smile. "That surprises you? You think I should be satisfied with Veerham, with Caprice and Adam, with my life. Well, old man, Veerham is a constant drain on my pocket —and if I'd known that, you would have been welcome to the place. I made a mistake when I married Caprice—we've never been happy. It isn't a marriage—it's a convenience. I often wonder why I didn't leave her years ago—I've had my opportunities—or why she didn't divorce me. Heaven knows I've given her enough cause. Adam's a nice child but I have little to do with him, you know—don't get on well together, that's the truth. He's too much like Caprice and she keeps him well under her influence. He'll probably grow up thinking his father a despicable character who chases other women and neglects his home and family."

"I can't visualise Caprice as the type of woman to deliberately influence your son against you," Luke said stiffly.

Cliff smiled. "Perhaps not. Maybe I imagine a good deal. Perhaps you know Caprice better than I do."

Luke stiffened. "That's most unlikely.

I've scarcely seen her more than a few times since you married her." He was not sure if there was any implication in his brother's words but he was immediately on his guard.

Cliff gestured lazily. "I never did care much for family ties. Just because we're brothers, there isn't any reason why I should inflict my family on you and you've never inflicted Margo or the girls on me. I've been away too much, I suppose." He paused briefly and Luke relaxed his guard a little but he was still suspicious of his brother's unusual loquaciousness. He went on: "But I said I envy you, Luke. Well, I do. Take Margo—she's good-looking and intelligent and she's reasonable. I wish Caprice were as reasonable. I admit I've given her a rotten deal—but she's never given me much, anyway. Your two girls— they're pretty little things and they're well behaved—Margo again, of course. Adam seems to dislike me—true I've never had much dealings with him but children never were attractive to me. I wanted a son for the title and the estate—all right, Caprice gave me one and I'm grateful. But there's no bond between Adam and I—he could

196

be a stranger's son except that casual affairs aren't in my wife's line." He grinned briefly. "Pity—she might be more tolerant of my affairs if she had a few of her own."

Luke said quickly: "I've always had the impression that Caprice is indifferent to your affairs with other women." He immediately regretted the words.

"I'm not implying that Caprice has ever been jealous. She doesn't love me so therefore she isn't jealous. But she doesn't like the humiliation of knowing that there are other women and she has a spiteful tongue at times." Luke said nothing to this. After a moment, Cliff went on: "I've never had much feeling for Veerham or this place—buildings don't interest me. But I can imagine now that one could be very happy here." He laughed. "I've never had time to be happy at Veerham—I don't spend a great deal of my life there. The place stifles me. I need new surroundings, new people, new pleasures—or I did. Now I'm beginning to feel that I've no roots. Veerham isn't a home. Caprice despises me and she certainly isn't a wife to me. Adam isn't the kind of son I'd visualised."

"You'll forgive me if I point out that the remedy lies in your own hands."

Cliff nodded. "I wouldn't have forgiven you if you told me that all these things are my own fault. But I think it's too late for remedies, Luke. I'm too old to change— I'm forty, you know. I started on the wrong path when I was only a boy—I've enjoyed my life and somehow I don't think I shall have any old age to enjoy. That doesn't worry me . . ." Suddenly he broke off and burst into loud laughter. "Your brandy is damn good stuff—but much too potent. I've talked too much. Most of it nonsense." He rose abruptly. "Shall we join Margo? She's a nice person—restful. I suppose I should have married a woman like her—someone who would be patient and understanding and content with the little I can give any woman."

Long after, Luke remembered his brother's words and he could find it possible to spare a brief pity for him. Obviously, he had regrets—even if he had laughed them off later with the poor excuse that the brandy had encouraged him to talk nonsense. Luke was glad that he had no regrets. His marriage was happy: he loved Margo; he was proud of his children.

He saw Caprice once between the time of Cliff's visit to the Hall—a visit that lengthened into several weeks for he seemed to find something which satisfied him at Mallingham and Margo made him very welcome—and the time of his death three years later.

It had been but a brief contact with Caprice. He had been in London and she had passed him in a taxi. She had pulled up the cab, dismissed it, and hurried after Luke. She was in London to make arrangements for Adam's new school and they only had time for coffee because she had arranged to meet some friends. But each treasured those few moments. They spoke of trivialities, of Cliff, of her son and Luke's children, of Margo and Mallingham, of their various recent activities—not once did they talk of themselves yet behind their light conversation ran the thread of their love for each other. When she finally left him in the taxi he had called for her, her hand lingered for a moment in his—then suddenly she leaned forward and kissed him fleetingly on the lips. He looked after the taxi as it drove away and knew that deep down in him, beneath the contentment of his life, still lived a yearning for what might have been if he and Caprice had been free to find happiness together.

Then one summer day, she arrived unexpectedly at the Hall and Adam was with her, a good-looking boy who was nearing thirteen.

Luke was out on his horse and Margo received Caprice and the boy with mild warmth and no little surprise at this unexpected descent.

But Caprice soon explained everything.

"I'm going to throw myself on your generosity," she said in her impetuous manner. "Cliff is seriously ill in Cannes. It's the school holidays and I don't know what to do with Adam. It isn't fair to take him with me to a sick-bed—will you have him here, Margo? I shall be eternally grateful."

"But of course. I'm sorry to hear about Cliff—what's wrong with him?"

Caprice shrugged. "I don't know. I had a cable from his friends. He must be very ill because he's never sent for me before

—he's been ill occasionally, you know, but usually I've known nothing about it at the time."

"You must be very anxious," Margo said gently.

Caprice glanced at her in surprise. "Anxious? No, I'm not. I'm not the type to pretend things I don't feel, Margo. It's my duty to go to Cannes—after all, I'm Cliff's wife. But I'm not exactly pleased about it. I was looking forward to this holiday with Adam."

Margo had her thoughts but she wisely kept them to herself. "Well, you know he'll be perfectly all right here. The girls will be delighted—they've seen so little of their cousin." She drew Adam to her and smoothed back the red-gold hair. "It will be very nice to have you with us for a while," she told him warmly.

He smiled at her. He was extremely well-mannered and very good-looking. "Thank you, Aunt Margo. You've got a lake, haven't you?"

"Yes, that's right. Do you like swimming?"

"Very much."

"If the weather is kind, you'll have

plenty of opportunities to try the lake then, my dear. I expect Francesca and Serena are there now—why not explore the place, Adam? You can't get lost. If you follow the path through the woods, it will take you to the lake."

He nodded. "May I, Mother?" He turned to Caprice.

"Yes, darling, of course." Her eyes glowed with love for this son. "I can trust you to behave yourself and obey your uncle and aunt?" She did not kiss him. "I will be back here as soon as I can, Adam."

He held out his hand to her and she took it. For a moment, they smiled at each other. Then with a brief but polite word of excuse, he left the room by the french windows and they heard his footsteps on the stone terrace steps.

"He's very handsome," Margo said. "And very polite." She rose and rang the bell. "I'll order some tea, Caprice—you aren't rushing away yet, surely?" For Caprice had risen involuntarily.

She sat down again. It had not been the thought of departure which caused that swift movement but the sound of Luke's voice in the hall. She said swiftly: "I'd love some tea, Margo."

A moment later, Luke came into the room. He was prepared to see Caprice for Vernon had told him that Lady Veerham was with his wife. But he still paused for a brief moment and his eyes were hungry with love as he looked at Caprice. Then he came further into the room, totally unaware that Margo had noticed that instinctive hesitation, had seen the look in his eyes.

"Caprice! This is a surprise!" he said. He approached and gave her his hand. She took it only briefly and then their hands unlinked.

"I'm on an errand of request," she said lightly. "I have to go to Cannes—Cliff is ill and has had me sent for. Adam's on holiday and I wondered if you'd be good enough to have him for a while. Margo has kindly consented—and Adam is already exploring his new surroundings."

"But of course Margo has consented," he said. "Did you expect we would turn the boy away? I'm glad you brought him here." He strode across to his wife and bent to touch her cheek with his lips. He never failed to salute her thus whenever he left or entered the house. It was a habit of long standing and Caprice with her keen perception, knew that it was motivated by nothing but habit.

"I've just rung for Vernon to order some tea," Margo said. She was composed and cool as always but the knowledge of that exchange of glances between her husband and Caprice burned in her breast.

"Good," he commended. He towered above her, hands thrust deep into his pockets to control the trembling which Caprice's presence had the power to bring about. How many years was it since these two women had been together in his presence? One, the woman he had married: the other, the woman he loved with every beat of his heart, every fibre of his being. "Well," he said. "We don't often have the pleasure of Caprice's company, do we, my dear?"

And just as well, was Margo's instinctive thought. But she replied lightly enough: "We don't see enough of your family at all, Luke. How strange it is that you should be so indifferent to Cliff's activities

—you don't seem at all disturbed about his illness now."

Luke shrugged. "Nothing to worry about. Cliff is a comparatively young man and he's never had a day's serious illness in his life." He turned to Caprice. "So you're chasing off to Cannes. Are you worried about Cliff? It isn't like you to desert Adam on his school holiday."

"Needs must when the devil drives," she said with a light tone. "I shall know that Adam is in good hands. Don't let him run wild, Luke—he's getting to the age when he wants new excitements. Just like his father." She spoke bitterly. She added in a different tone: "I'm not really worried about Cliff but I imagine he must be very ill for his friends to cable me so urgently."

They sat over tea for some time and Margo strove to keep the conversation on Adam and his school and his interests. She did not like the odd feeling that she was an outsider whenever Luke and Caprice exchanged remarks. As trivial as those remarks were, she felt that they forgot her very existence when they spoke to each other. It reminded her vividly of her wedding day when she had experienced the same feeling—a memory she had almost forgotten which occasionally returned to torment her. She did not know why she was so concerned about Caprice. Or if she did know, she was certainly determined not to formulate it into words or admit to anything which might bring her pain.

At last, Caprice rose. "My son is probably wallowing in the lake or getting himself filthy in the woods," she said lightly. "We've made our farewells so I won't go in search of him. I do appreciate your kindness, Margo. I hope I won't have to leave him on your hands for very long. I'll let you know how Cliff gets on. I must be moving now, though—I've a lot to do yet." She moved over to the window and looked out across the gardens. "How beautiful this place is in the summer—almost as lovely as it is in the spring. At least, the water will be warmer, Luke." And she threw him a laughing glance. Then in the sudden silence that took possession of the room, she hastily gathered her wandering thoughts and moved away from the window.

"I'll come to the door with you," Luke

offered. He paused while Caprice thanked Margo again and bestowed a light kiss on the cool cheek which his wife offered. The the atmosphere was frigid and when he stood with Caprice by her car, he said ruefully, "You've let me in for some explanations now, my dear."

"I'm sorry, Luke—it was foolish of me. I had forgotten Margo." She smiled up at him. It was a beautiful smile, containing love and tenderness and warmth. "I'm afraid I always do forget Margo when I'm with you, Luke."

He caught her hand and gripped it with powerful pressure, glad of the brief contact, longing for more. "I love you," he said vehemently, urgently and yet perforce in little more than a whisper.

"Bless you," she replied quietly. Then she released her hand and slipped into the driving seat. With a brief wave, she drove away down the long, winding drive to the gates.

A little hesitantly, Luke went back to the drawing-room, forming explanations in his mind, wondering how Margo would approach the subject, and yet not once feeling even a momentary anger or impatience against Caprice for her folly.

Margo looked up from her sewing as he went into the room. He threw himself into an armchair and waited for her questions. But she said nothing for a long time. At last, he could wait no longer and he said abruptly: "I expect you were surprised by what Caprice said about the Hall in spring. I had forgotten—in fact, I never even thought to mention it to you, my dear, it was so unimportant to me. It was a long time ago—do you remember when you stayed at Liscott with the girls for a week before Michael was born? Caprice came here unexpectedly and stayed a few hours." Why did you not say days? he demanded of his own tongue. He knew his voice was uneven and certainly not very convincing. "It wasn't a very warm day," he hurried on, "but she had the whim to try the lake—as she remarked, the water was very cold."

"Rather a long way to come—from Veerham—just for a few hours," Margo said and her voice was cool. No trace of anger or of doubt. No warmth either.

Luke laughed. "Caprice is unpredict-

able—I expect she was bored or restless."
Margo made no reply. After a few
minutes, he leaped to his feet. "I think I'll
take a walk down to the lake and see how
Adam is getting on with the girls—if he's
with them, that is. I hope he makes friends
with them."

"I should imagine he's very reserved,"
Margo said. "I think he's rather a
charming child—more like Cliff than
Caprice."

Was there a barb in that remark? Luke
wondered as he strode swiftly across the
lawn towards the woods. He felt that he
would never understand Margo—never
pierce the armour of her cool withdrawal
and quiet serenity. Had she really accepted
his words at their face value? Was she as
undisturbed as she seemed? He had been
a fool to rush in with explanations. Far
better to wait for a question which might
never have come. Perhaps he had imagined
the sudden tensing of the atmosphere after
Caprice had thrown those words into the
pool of conversation. He might have
unnecessarily brought up the subject
again.

During the weeks that followed, Margo

made no mention of the new knowledge and fear that lived within her. She felt it would serve no purpose to batter Luke's defence with questions to which she would never get very satisfactory replies. For many years she had suspected that someone else's image was cherished in Luke's heart. She had always known that he did not love her as a man should love his wife but knowing him to be faithful and reliable and affectionate, she had been content. They had been very happy together and she was grateful for this happiness. She did not know that it was Caprice who owned his heart but she had suspected very faintly and vaguely for some time. Now she was convinced that it was so but she did not mean to do anything about it. Luke was apparently content with matters as they stood and certainly she was.

Adam seemed perfectly happy at the Hall. He had settled in well and seemed to be one of the family. Margo liked him: he got on very well with Serena despite the difference in their ages and they spent most of their waking hours together; he seemed to hold the serene and self-possessed Francesca a little in awe and she made no secret of her indifference to him. He loved the small Michael and he and Serena took the child everywhere with them unless their excursions were likely to endanger health and limb.

His golden skin tanned to a deep bronze. His red-gold hair was more gold from frequent exposure to the sun. He put on weight and seemed to grow taller with every day. He was not so solemn and certainly not so well-behaved. Not that he was actively naughty but he was more child-like and Margo encouraged this healthy enthusiasm for children's pursuits. She imagined that the boy had led a strange life with his mother's doting love on one side and his father's indifference on the other.

Caprice was away for eight weeks. Then Luke received a cable from her which told him that his brother had died and she was returning to England a few days after the funeral. As he had loved France so much and had never been completely happy at Veerham, she had decided against bringing his body home to the family vault and he was being buried in Cannes.

When she came to Mallingham, Luke was shocked by her pallor and the loss of weight. She told him in a flat voice that Cliff had indeed been very ill, that she had nursed him throughout the eight weeks he had lain supine, sometimes delirious, mainly unconscious, and that it had been a relief when he finally had died one night. Just before he died, he had recovered consciousness long enough to apologise for the life he had given her and to beg her to keep up Veerham for Adam.

It surprised Luke that his brother in his last moments should have turned his thoughts both to his wife and his son—but then he remembered Cliff's almost forgotten words to him at the time of Michael's christening and he wondered if remorse and regret had eaten into his brother's soul during the last few years. Certainly as he lay dying and perhaps reviewing his life, he could have found little cause for satisfaction. Aware of Caprice's quiet ministrations and untiring vigil, he might have recalled the days when they were both young and newly in love— a love which did not last under the stresses of marriage. Maybe he regretted the many affairs in which he had indulged since his marriage: the frequent sojourns abroad and his consequent neglect of Caprice and Adam and the beautiful Veerham; his apparent indifference for convention, his waywardness and many follies.

But now he was dead and he could be forgiven his many faults and sins. His thirteen year old son was now Lord Veerham in his stead and Luke was well pleased to learn that throughout the years Caprice had fostered in her son a love for his majestic and beautiful home and encouraged him to discover many historical anecdotes about his home and family. He received the news of his father's death with apparent unconcern. Luke wondered if the boy realised the importance of his new position, the wealth he would inherit when he was twenty-one, the many duties incumbent on him as Lord Veerham. For the time being, while he was still but a boy, the management of his affairs and estates fell on Luke's shoulders as he discovered from Cliff's will and Caprice was grateful to him for taking all the cares and anxieties from her shoulders.

Adam went back to school and Caprice

took a flat in London, taking up the threads of her old life and former friends, filling her days with engagements and pleasures. Luke saw much of her for there were plenty of excuses to meet her for lunch or for a cocktail if only to discuss the estate or Adam's welfare or education. Caprice was free now and if there were not Margo and his children to consider he knew that he would ask her to marry him. But he was bound to Margo and it was impossible to seek his freedom. Caprice refused to listen to any suggestions he might put forward for their chance of happiness together. She was not an immoral woman and she would not encourage Luke to be unfaithful to his wife. She was happy in a quietly peaceful way with her flat, her many friends and social activities, her interest in Adam. During his school holidays she took him abroad or went with him to Veerham and they were always together. Once or twice she brought Adam to the Hall but possibly she sensed that Margo, for all her composure and ease of manner, her charm and kindness, resented her presence at the Hall. Aware that Adam was happy staying with Luke and his family, she soon made some excuse to return to London, leaving the boy at Mallingham for a few weeks of his holiday. Adam was her first consideration and it seemed that she had put aside all thoughts of her own happiness, all the longings of her own love for Luke, and all the painful reminders of the past. She never mentioned Cliff or her marriage again. She was still a comparatively young woman and very beautiful and she did not lack male company either in London or when she was at Veerham or abroad. Luke often dreaded the news that she intended to marry again as the years slipped by and her name appeared more frequently in the society magazines and society columns of the newspapers, always linked with some man or other.

His own life went on as smoothly as ever. His children were growing up. Margo was growing older and betraying it a little. His marriage was still bound round with bonds of steel which were not actively uncomfortable bonds despite his love for Caprice and the hope—fainter now—that one day they would find happiness together. It seemed that they would have to wait until eternity but his love never faltered and he gained support from Caprice's brave front to the world, the undying love which lived in her being yet must always be denied and concealed for fear of hurting someone but themselves.

11

LUKE surveyed the scene with a satisfied smile. He had certainly given Francesca a party worthy of her sweetness and beauty and popularity. She passed by him at that moment, dancing in a man's arms, and she flashed him a swift, sweet smile—a smile so like her mother's that he felt a brief regret for the passing years.

Francesca at eighteen was very like Margo when he had first known her: her golden hair was swept up into a knot of curls at the back of her head and caught with a glittering jet brooch. She was too young to wear black, he thought, but it had been her own choice and nothing had been denied her for this occasion—her birthday ball and official debut into society. He could not deny that the black gown suited her tall slenderness to perfection and enhanced the beauty of her bright hair, the perfect pink and white complexion, the blue of her eyes. Yet with it all was that aloof reserve, the quiet air of withdrawal, the serenity which she had inherited from Margo and which her mother had never lost in all these years.

His affectionate gaze sought and found Margo. The gold of her hair was silvery now but she was still a young woman—not yet forty-four. It had betrayed those silver strands ever since Michael's birth—and he was a tall, handsome boy of ten now, home for this occasion from his school and standing by the side of his mother.

Margo wore a blue and silver dress which sparkled in the illumination from the chandeliers and revealed shoulders white and smooth, a little plumper now. Though she talked eagerly and vivaciously to her friends—more vivacious than her usual quiet manner—Luke knew that she was very conscious of her son and occasionally her hand rested on his shoulder and once or twice she turned her head to give him a smile such as she had never bestowed on any other. She was not only proud of Michael: she loved him with an ardent depth of emotion which she had never shown to the girls or to her husband.

Since his birth, all her interest and warmth and affection had been given to Michael —never neglecting the girls but still not displaying the same interest. If she still loved Luke, she never betrayed it. They lived together like good friends and companions but with every passing year they had drifted apart—emotionally, mentally and physically. They had never been spiritually attuned so he did not notice the lack of this—but the other rifts in their marriage had bewildered and grieved him until he had learned to accept the situation. They were such small rifts —possibly only he and Margo were aware of them because once they had been very close—not enough to shatter the even tenor of their life together so that they were actively unhappy or dissatisfied but both were vaguely aware that they had not achieved all their dreams—although no word was ever spoken of this feeling of failure.

The big house hummed now with music, conversation and laughter, the tinkle of glasses, the shuffle of soft slippers on the paved floor of the hall which had been turned into a ballroom for the occasion. It was many years since the Hall had known so many guests under its roof —many years since a Fortune had entertained so lavishly as this, but Francesca was a daughter to love and be proud of and he felt that nothing should be denied her on this splendid occasion. The place was ablaze with light and colour. He was amused by the dresses that his daughters' friends wore and wondered at the trend of fashion—but they were attractive and Luke had no resentment against the modern young people or their somewhat doubtful way of life. The young men seemed to him much as young men had always seemed—perhaps a few of them affected a strange cut of tailoring but that too was modern, and was no indication of a lack in their integrity or character or morality. His own conventional black and white found a response in many of his contemporaries who were present. He met Richard Hamilton's eyes and nodded briefly. Richard smiled across the ballroom and his smile indicated that once they too had been as youthful and careless and pleasure-loving as these young people. Richard had proved a good friend throughout the years—staunch and loyal, reliable and trustworthy, always eager to hear one's arguments and opinions or minor grumbles.

Luke raised a hand to his own red-gold hair. He was vain enough to be pleased that it was still as thick and bright as ever. No trace of silver touched its waving mass. He looked down at himself and pulled in the bulge of his stomach—a very slight bulge, fortunately. He was still very slim and handsome. Only his face betrayed the advancing years. Little lines were in profusion about his eyes and traced heavily by his mouth. His chin had grown a little heavy. He was no longer a young man—indeed, he preferred not to remember that within a few years he would be fifty!

"Daddy, darling, how solemn you look!"

That was Serena who had dragged her partner to a standstill before him and raised laughing eyes to her beloved father. She was a refreshing picture, the hair, which was the same colour as his own, curling riotously over a small head, her eyes innocent and filled with laughter, her face piquantly lovely, her slim body encased in a dress of ivory which enhanced her beauty. She was very mature for sixteen and he felt a warm surge of love mingling with regretful sadness that she too was growing up and beyond him; one day soon she would replace him in her heart with another man—possibly her present partner, Adam. Luke's love for this younger daughter was as staunch and passionate as ever. She never failed him in any way. Margo could claim Francesca and Michael for her own: as long as he had Serena, he was perfectly content.

He smiled at her. "Well, my pet—are you enjoying yourself?"

"Very much," she assured him. She lifted her bright eyes to her partner's face. "Adam is my faithful partner, as always."

Adam—the son of Cliff and Caprice. A tall, fine-looking young man, now almost twenty: he had the Fortune hair and build but his dark, glowing eyes and mature vitality were all Caprice. Luke was very fond of this sensitive young man and sensed the qualities within him. He was worthy of his ancient name and title and estates. Not yet twenty-one, he was still proving himself capable of supervising the estate management and he was an apt and ready pupil under Luke, always willing to take advice but occasionally startling the older man with a shrewd decision which invariably proved the right one.

He wondered what would come of his friendship with Serena. The girl was devoted to her cousin: it was almost adoration and there were times when Luke wished it were shared more equally among the many young men she knew in the district. But Adam and Serena were inseparable when it was possible. If he was not at the Hall, then Serena went to Veerham. If he was in London, so was she, staying with Caprice at her flat. He was studying at one of Oxford's universities and during term time, Serena frequently went there for weekends or for university social functions. Caprice was very fond of Serena and seemed to encourage the friendship between the girl and her son. Luke and Margo did not interfere. They knew the two were fond of each other; that they could be trusted not to place too romantic an interpretation on their feeling for each other at this stage when both were so young; and that Serena would never come to any harm with the cousin she adored.

Luke smiled now at Adam. "We're interrupting your studies again. How are you getting on at Oxford, anyway?"

"Oh, I keep my nose to the grindstone, sir." He was a courteous and charming young man. Luke often wondered how Cliff had managed to father such a sensitive and intelligent individual. But perhaps he had inherited these traits from his mother. Adam looked around the big hall. "This is a wonderful show, sir—everyone seems to be enjoying themselves. Francesca is a real stunner, isn't she?"

Luke nodded his agreement. "I suppose it won't be long before it's Serena's turn. Daughters are a great expense. This kind of thing is supposed to get them off your hands and into the arms of some eligible young man—but I'm not at all sure that I want to lose either of them." He sighed briefly. "You young people grow up so fast."

Serena slipped her hand in his arm and raised up on her toes to kiss his cheek. "Darling—you won't lose me for years and years and years. By then, you'll be glad to hand me over to some nice young man."

"Me, for instance," grinned Adam.

Luke pulled thoughtfully at his lower lip. "It wouldn't be a bad idea to keep Veerham in the family that way," he said teasingly. "I've always wanted it myself— the next best thing is seeing my grandson in possession of the place."

"You're way ahead of me, sir," Adam put in quickly, and a slight flush stained his cheeks.

Luke smiled reassuringly. "Where's your mother, Adam?"

He did not need to put the question for even as Adam replied lightly: "I believe she's in the drawing-room imbibing champagne," Luke felt the familiar tingle of stirring blood in his veins and he glanced across the ballroom to see Caprice coming from the room, glancing back over her shoulder with her face alight with laughter. Then she came on to mingle with the crowd of dancers. For a moment she was obscured by a dancing couple then their eyes met across the space of the hall and held for a long moment.

Serena intercepted that speaking

exchange of glances and she tugged suddenly at Adam's hand. "Come on—I love this tune. Let's dance."

Willingly, he caught hold of her slim waist and swung her into the movements of the dance. For a brief moment, Luke looked after them, envying their youth and freedom and happiness. Then Caprice was by his side and she laid a hand on his arm. They still sought the joy of this occasional contact. "They make a wonderful couple," she said in that low, husky voice which still had the power to stir his emotion.

He looked down at her. She was still beautiful though her temples were white now, distinguished wings which seemed to add to her attraction. "Yes," he agreed. "One day I think I shall lose my Serena to your son."

She laughed softly, a fluting laugh. "That will be rather ironic."

He caught her hand and pressed it tightly. "You never seem to get any older, Caprice," he said impulsively. "It isn't possible that Adam is your son."

She smiled slowly, bewitchingly. "Do you really doubt it? My dear, I'm forty-five."

"And as beautiful as you were at twenty-five," he said quietly.

She gently took her hand from his. "We aren't alone," she reminded him. "We've seldom given cause for gossip—don't let's begin now." She smiled up at him again. "Let's go on to the terrace, my dear. I've been caught up with stupid, chattering people all evening. Now I want to talk to you."

He followed her without hesitation on to the stone terrace. Fairy lights were erected about the gardens and their colourful illuminations gave their surroundings an enchanting beauty. Caprice walked with rustling skirts and a familiar lithe grace to a seat which overlooked the gardens. She sat down and the folds of her rich scarlet dress billowed about her. He stood looking down at her then he sat beside her and captured her hand again, this time without rebuff or rebuke.

"Caprice," he said urgently. "Perhaps I'm too old to talk like a lover—but I still love you. You know that, don't you?"

Her eyes were very tender. "Dear Luke. Of course I know it—I'm as thankful now as I was ten years ago. And you aren't too old—you and I will never be old, my dear —not while we love each other."

He was suddenly sad. "The many years that we've wasted, Caprice. All the years of loving each other and being apart. There are times when I regret that we didn't say to hell with everything and find our happiness together. What would we have wanted of the world if we'd had each other, my darling? We could have gone abroad—rented a small place—left the world behind." He spoke urgently and yet with that trace of hushed sadness that tore at her heart.

She hushed him gently. "The world is always with us, Luke. There have always been too many obstacles in the way of our happiness. Adam. Margo and your children . . ."

He interrupted her sharply. "The main obstacle was Cliff—and he's been dead seven years. Do you realise that I would have given up everything for you—Margo, the girls, Michael and the Hall, my friends? I would have begged Margo to divorce me and I would have married you —but you wouldn't listen to any suggestions I ever made."

"We've no right to happiness at other people's expense," she said quietly. "Divorce is an ugly word, my dear. It would always taint our life together—reflect on Adam and your three attractive offspring—and certainly would be poor return to Margo for all her loyalty and love through the years. No, Luke darling—I'm just not made that way—I won't take happiness with the full knowledge that I'm hurting someone else by doing so."

His fingers were clamped like steel over hers but she did not wince or try to withdraw them. "You don't love me, Caprice," he accused. "You never have. You've amused yourself with teasing me and playing on my emotions and revenging Cliff for his treatment of you—you've never loved me as I love you . . ."

She cut in and her tone was icy. "If you can really think such things of me, Luke, it would be as well if I did not love you so much."

He raised her fingers to his lips, instantly contrite. "My darling, I'm sorry." He would have gone on but she hushed him suddenly with her fingers hard on his lips. Beneath them in the garden stood two people talking quietly. On the still air their voices rose clearly and they were apparently unaware that anyone was on the terrace above for Luke and Caprice had been murmuring in low tones. Luke stiffened. He immediately recognised his daughter's voice and the deeper, pleasant tones of Adam. Caprice inclined her head a little to catch the words the better and her dark eyes were glowing in the soft light. She seemed agitated but Serena's light words with the undercurrent of anxiety were enough to agitate anyone closely connected with her remarks.

"I've always known how Daddy feels about her," Serena said stubbornly.

"You must be mistaken," Adam replied but he was not very dogmatic.

"Adam!" The tone was reproachful. "Men are so unobservant," she added scornfully. "I know that Caprice and Daddy are in love—it's written all over them. One has only to see the way he looks at her—and it's true enough that he's often at the flat when he goes up to London. You know that, Adam. How often have we found them having tea together or talking over a drink or just on the way to the theatre?"

Adam sounded uncomfortable. "Don't make it sound *so wrong*, Serena. I refuse to believe that either my mother or Uncle Luke is capable of an unpleasantly grimy affair unknown to anyone."

"Adam, I didn't imply that it was either unpleasant or grimy. I merely said that they're in love—I think they always have been. Even as a small girl, I knew that Daddy didn't love Mummy—they've always been very happy but that one necessary spark has never existed between them. I can sense it between Caprice and Daddy. I'm not condemning them," she added in a sophisticated tone. "After all, this isn't the Dark Ages. I think it would be an excellent thing if Mummy divorced Daddy and he married Caprice."

"My God!" murmured Luke involuntarily and felt Caprice's fingers tighten on his arm. To hear his youngest daughter calmly discussing divorce and his love for Caprice hurt him to the heart. He had always determined that his children should be untouched by his love for a woman not his wife. Caprice had always pointed out that the children must never be tainted by divorce. Yet here were their respective son and daughter discussing the whole idea with apparently no condemnation and much approval.

For Adam said thoughtfully, "That certainly seems to be the answer. But is Aunt Margo the type to give your father his freedom without quibbling?"

"Oh, Mummy would agree to anything as long as she had her precious Michael." She laughed softly. "If our much respected parents did get married, Adam, you could be Daddy's son—he's terribly fond of you."

"That would make us brother and sister in a way, I suppose," he said and there was a note of rue in his voice. There was a long silence and Luke looked at Caprice and gestured with his head towards the house. Surely they had heard enough and it was not the thing to eavesdrop with deliberate intent. Caprice nodded without speaking and began to rise. Then Adam said loudly and with apparent and real dread: "Mother told me that she knew Uncle Luke before I was born—I suppose that's natural enough as Father and Uncle

Luke were brothers. But, Serena, do you think they loved each other then?"

"Yes, I do," Serena replied stoutly. She had a romantic turn of mind and she had apparently given the subject much thought.

"You don't think—I mean, my father and Uncle Luke were very alike—who could prove whether I resembled Father or Uncle Luke most? I mean—Serena, you don't think . . ."

She finished for him eagerly at first and then with a note of dismay as she realised the intent. "That you could be Daddy's son? Oh, Adam—you would be my brother then—and we couldn't be married!"

Luke wondered if Adam took his daughter into his arms and kissed her for his voice was a little muffled and tense when he spoke again. "I hope it isn't so, my darling—but we'll have to find out. I'll talk to Uncle Luke—he's the type of person one can talk to on equal terms. I must know—I'm determined to marry you. If that's impossible, then we'll live together, Serena. For I love you and I won't give you up for any reason on earth."

Caprice rose abruptly. "I can't stand any more of this!" she exclaimed harshly and walked away to the far end of the terrace. Luke followed her and slipped his arm about her shoulders. "Those poor children," she said with sorrow in her voice. She caught her breath sharply and he bent his head to kiss away a tear which streaked her cheek, gleaming in the pale illumination of the gardens.

"Those fortunate children," he amended. "You and I know that there's no reason on earth why Adam should have to give up Serena. They're cousins—nothing more. I'm not particularly keen on the marriage of cousins but they've been devoted to each other since childhood and who could deny them their happiness." He sighed briefly. "I've never had the happiness I've always wanted with you—I'm not going to stand in the way of our children, Caprice."

She recovered her composure. "Who would think that Serena was so perceptive? And obviously Adam has noticed things too but never mentioned them—did you notice how readily he accepted Serena's explanations? How can we be safe, my darling, when mere children can see through our guard?"

"Do you think Adam will really have a man to man talk with me about this fear of his that I might be his father?"

Caprice laughed. "I'm sure he will. He's very direct, you know—and he hates pretence."

"He's definitely your son," Luke said. "You don't seem very concerned that Adam and Serena seem to know the workings of our innermost hearts as well as we do."

"I'm not concerned. They are not children—they are certainly not fools. Is it likely that they will run around telling everyone their suspicions? I think it's rather touching that they're so obviously on our side—and yet I'm capable of sympathy for Margo that her own daughter would gladly see her cast aside in order that her father should have long-awaited happiness."

"Should we take their advice, darling?" he pressed her. "After all, if these modern young people are not shocked with the idea of divorce, why should we throw up our hands in horror and expect our contemporaries to banish us from society? Shall I ask Margo to divorce me? Our marriage has been on weak foundations for some years now—I can't believe that she would refuse my request. I want to marry you, Caprice. I've always wanted to marry you. I might have tried many times to persuade you to come away with me—but I've always had marriage in the back of my mind, the hope that Margo would find out and divorce me, the desire to call you my wife."

"It's a pity you could not have been more honest with the woman who is your wife," a cold voice said behind him and he turned his head in shocked dismay to meet Margo's calm, cold eyes.

Caprice moved forward instantly to face Margo. "You heard?" she asked quietly, almost tenderly.

"Everything," Margo said with amazing composure. "The flights of fancy of those two children—and then the confirmation from the lips of two adults who should know better than to discuss their private emotions at such a time. Anyone could have overheard—and I might have suffered a sight more humiliation than I am at present."

"Margo—you must let me explain," Luke said quickly, desperately, stepping forward in his turn.

"Of course I will, Luke," she replied smoothly. "But not right now. You have a duty to your guests—I expect we have both been missed. Tomorrow we can talk this over."

"You're prepared to be reasonable?" Luke asked eagerly.

She threw him a mildly reproachful glance. "I think no one could call me unreasonable, Luke. Now—you'll forgive us, Caprice—but we must go back to the ballroom. Will you give me your arm, Luke?"

Obediently yet still a little stunned by the unexpected turn of events, the surprising calm of his wife in the face of what surely must be devastating knowledge, Luke offered his arm to Margo and she entered the house by his side while Caprice stood watching them, pale, her dark eyes glittering in the pallor of her face, her back against the stone balustrade of the terrace as though she needed the support, her whole body trembling with the ordeal of the morrow seeming very grim and yet hopeful. Margo had taken it very well. Perhaps she would gladly consent to the dissolution of her marriage. Perhaps she too had always known how matters were between her husband and Cliff's wife—she was a shrewdly perceptive woman even if Luke was not aware quite how perceptive she could be.

After all these long years—every passing year an eternity—was it possible that she and Luke would be granted the chance to find happiness together? Their love had never faltered in any way yet it was twenty years since that meeting at Veerham when each had fallen in love with the other on sight and concealed it with admirable dexterity. Twenty years—each day seeming to drag at the time and yet looking back now it seemed to Caprice that it was but a few months since she had been that wild, impulsive and passionate girl.

12

MARGO moved among her guests and none guessed at the anguish in her being for she was cool and composed and gracious as ever. She had been born with this gift of concealing her innermost emotions and it proved a very useful asset. How many times had she felt inwardly like death? When her heart had battered against the cruel cage of self-control and the blood had run cold in her veins. The time when Michael had been found in the lake, lying face down at the water's edge, having stumbled and hit his head on a sharp stone. Only by chance had Adam come across the child that day and dragged him from the water, carrying him in his arms to the house. She had run from the drawing-room at his call and the blood had drained from her heart and every pulse was stilled at the sight of her son with his waxen pallor and the blood streaking his brow and staining his red-gold hair. But she had quietly walked down the stone steps, taken Michael into her own arms and carried him into the house, requesting Adam to telephone for Heath and to keep the girls away from the house for the time being. Self-control had been very useful then.

Going further back to the time when Caprice had brought her son here before leaving for France to nurse Cliff—Luke had not been sufficiently on his guard and for a brief moment his eyes had revealed his innermost emotions. Margo then had wanted to cry out against the truth which struck at her heart—but she had calmly made some remark and given away no hint of the turmoil within her. Times without number, she had been tempted to probe into Luke's feelings for Caprice—a casual word or question—a slighting statement—it would have been easy for another woman but not for Margo with her innate acceptance and honesty. She could not deny the truth but she did not want confirmation from her husband's lips.

Many years back now, when she had returned from Liscott with the two girls —before Michael's birth—and meeting Richard Hamilton had heard him make some casual remark about Lady Veerham's stay at the Hall. She had hardly heard anything else he said and as quickly but as discreetly as possible she had left him— and she had never told anyone that she knew of Caprice's visit and its duration. For days she had waited for Luke to mention it and when he did not this was evidence in full of his guilt—but never did she accuse him or seek to trap him into admission. Instead, she buried her head in the sand and padded herself around with memories of Luke's kindness and consideration, his affection, their happy home life, his many good points and qualities. She would not let herself believe that he was capable of faithlessness. She watched him with the children. She studied him carefully when she told him of the child she expected. She remembered his anxiety for her when Michael was born and his relief that both she and the boy were all right. None of these things held the timbre of a guilty man and she knew that her trust in him was justified.

Gradually, she found it in her heart to admire him. For Margo knew beyond all doubt that her husband loved Caprice as a man only loved once in his life. She knew too that she had no complaint against him but for this love. She had not suffered in any way for he cared for her and did not hesitate to show his affection. He had proved himself to be a wonderful husband, a loyal companion, an excellent father. Yet loving Caprice he must surely long for the happiness she could give him. Apart from the first brief storm of jealousy, Margo knew that Caprice gave Luke nothing but her heart—and she admired the woman too. She was strictly fair and she gave her admiration gladly and willingly, knowing it to be well merited. She wondered if she would have been as strong in a similar situation. Richard Hamilton had once accidentally betrayed that he was in love with her —another time when self-control was very necessary—and Margo did not deceive herself. If she had loved Richard in return, then she would have betrayed Luke without hesitaion. But she did not love him.

It is no commendation to resist temptation when the wish to surrender doesn't exist. It is when one resists temptation against the need and desire of one's heart that strength of will power and resistance is commendable. Margo was aware of this —so she did not consider her own restraint to be at all remarkable—but she willingly applauded Luke and Caprice for their resistance to a temptation that must have been often very great.

She found certain consolation in her son and she had turned to him more and more. She knew she could not offer Luke his freedom for several reasons. One obvious one was that he had never confessed his love for Caprice and she was incapable of admitting that she knew of it—for after all it was a certainty of the heart rather than of reason or knowledge. Another was the children: she had a strong distaste for broken marriages in which children were made to suffer—perhaps when they were older, she would find it possible to give Luke his freedom—if he still wanted it. These had been the arguments she put up.

Margo did not sleep at all that night. To be sure it was the early hours before the many guests departed, before the excellent orchestra packed up their instruments and left, before the excited Francesca and Serena could be induced to go to bed—

and she was free to seek the cool peace and quiet comfort of her bedroom.

She threw herself on her bed and buried her face in her arms. In that moment she was not the ageing mother of growing children but a young girl with an ache in her heart that seemed to possess her whole body. But tears refused to spill—she had never found it easy to cry over anything.

So at last she rose and carefully slipped out of the blue and silver gown. She put on a dressing-gown and sat down to brush her blonde hair with long, rhythmic strokes.

She heard the sounds of Luke's steps in the passage and knew that he had come up from the library where he had gone to smoke a last pipe. Her hand stilled and her eyes flew to the door. She wondered if he would knock and come into her room —but although he hesitated by her door, as she knew by the break in his footsteps, he did not knock and a moment later she heard the quiet closing of his bedroom door.

Then Margo rose from her dressing-table and went over to the window. She drew back the heavy drapes and looked out over the gardens. Down below one of the servants moved on the terrace, probably clearing up empty glasses and plates and sweeping up cigarette stubs. He worked by the light from the drawing-room windows. The gardens were still illuminated by the pretty fairy lights—but even as Margo looked at them, they faded into blackness in one sudden instant. Somewhere, someone had flicked the switch which destroyed their pretty, shallow beauty.

So a light had gone out in her heart, Margo thought bleakly. Tonight, all the barriers had fallen. She had heard Adam and Serena discussing their respective mother and father with cool, decisive voices—and she had been stunned. Then she had listened deliberately to the exchange between Luke and Caprice. She was not ashamed of the eavesdropping for now she knew exactly where she stood. Luke wanted his freedom to marry Caprice.

Did her arguments still carry water? She knew now openly and without any doubt, having heard it from Luke's own lips, that he was in love with Caprice and had been for many years.

Francesca was eighteen years old. She was a young woman with an impenetrable reserve: all her life she had modelled herself on her mother and this had not been difficult for she had inherited a great many of Margo's traits. Margo doubted if the scandal of a divorce would touch Francesca very deeply—she was a modern and many of her friends thought nothing of broken marriages. She was self-sufficient, loving her parents only mildly: she would not be heartbroken if they no longer lived together under the same roof. No doubt she would marry—she was beautiful and popular and the young always had unshakable faith in their ability to succeed where others fail.

Serena? She adored her father—but Margo had heard her remarks that evening and she did not need to ask what her youngest daughter thought of divorce. The child was all in favour of Luke marrying Adam's mother. With startling precocity she had torn away the veil which had always discreetly hidden the unswerving love between Luke and Caprice. No doubt she was quite truthful when she said that she had known for years. She had always been exceptionally close to Luke and perhaps she had sensed that she had a rival for his affections apart from her mother. She had her own life apparently mapped out. She meant to marry Adam—it would not hurt her in any way if divorce touched her life for it would merely glance off her own happiness, which was always a shield for the world's hurts.

Margo dismissed the fear which Serena had stirred into life in Adam's heart. Without an instant's doubt she knew that Caprice had never been Luke's mistress—either before Adam was born or after. Adam was Cliff's son—and there was no impediment to a marriage between him and Serena except the old-fashioned prejudice to marriage between cousins and Margo felt that this could be cast aside in this case.

Michael? He was very much her son. Luke loved the boy and sought his company when he was at home. Yet between Margo and her son existed a rare bond which she knew must never be broken. He was a sensitive child and he was the one who would suffer most if his parents dissolved their marriage. But surely Luke would agree to the boy being with her during his holidays. Of course she would make no objection to Luke's occasional contact with Michael. It was unlikely that Luke would present any difficulties—and neither would she. They were both adult, logical people and they had always been friends and companions. They must discuss this affair from a friendly viewpoint and she must relinquish him to Caprice without a murmur of protest. She had known all his loyalty and affection and staunch companionship for twenty years. He had never failed her in any way but that of love—and strangely she had never felt the lack of anything in him. Her own love for him had been deep and powerful and ample enough for two. She believed firmly that to love is to want to give and to go on giving with one's whole heart. Her love was of this quality. She had given Luke everything of which she was capable—and she had never demanded anything in return which was not within his power to give. This was possibly the secret of her contentment in her marriage—and the reason why Luke had been happy. For she knew that he had been happy, despite the love for Caprice which must always have possessed him. Now she must give Luke the ultimate gift —freedom from the bonds which prevented him from finding happiness with Caprice.

Margo felt now that she should have been generous enough to do this when Cliff's death had freed Caprice—then it had been impossible but now she felt that it could be done.

She had been happy: she would always have her memories and no doubt she would always have Michael; she might even re-marry for she was still comparatively young and attractive, her body was still slim and eye-catching, and twenty years of marriage and domestic life had not dulled her intellect or her interest in other things. She actually smiled to herself as she thought that one day she might marry Richard—he had been very patient and always kind and charming. She liked him very much and they had many interests in common. They had known each other for years . . .

She thought of Caprice and the many men who had been linked with her name since Cliff's death. She had enjoyed her freedom and no doubt had found a certain amount of happiness even if she could not give full rein to her love for Luke. Margo recalled the words of those two children in the garden and wondered how often Luke had lunched or dined with Caprice, taken her to the theatre or down to the coast in his car. It really didn't matter. Gossip had never reached her ears so she had never been humiliated. Mallingham was a long way from London and her friends evidently knew nothing of the affair between Luke and Caprice—so she had not suffered in that respect.

She had a great capacity for generosity and she felt no jealousy at the thought of Luke escorting Caprice around town, spending days in her company and long hours at the flat. Surely they had earned the right to a little happiness.

She thought of Caprice's life with Cliff and knew it had never been a happy one. At first she had been inclined to blame Caprice for the failure of the marriage— but throughout the years she had learned from Luke what a difficult, restless and inconsiderate boor his brother had been. As she grew to know Caprice better—and to feel sincere affection for her—she could sympathise with her lack of happiness with Cliff and assess accurately at whose feet lay the blame.

Centuries earlier, Margo would have made a wonderful martyr—resigned—eager, indeed—to give up everything for the sake of something which she firmly believed—and now she firmly believed that Luke and Caprice loved beyond the understanding of the average person and that they had been patient long enough, deserving now the rightful reward for their patience and loyalty to their love.

Certainly she was not without a certain amount of pain for what she was giving up herself. She loved Luke very much. Her love had been consistent and true for over twenty years. She had been a good and faithful wife—and when she thought that her demonstrative affection burdened him with guilt because of his love for another woman, then she had taught herself to be cool and reserved and withdrawn so that she should not add to his pain.

She could scarcely visualise a future when she would no longer be Luke's wife and mistress of his lovely home. She would always be the mother of his children but they were growing up so quickly— growing up and away from the family ties which were never so strong as they had been in earlier generations. Children were independent at an early age and perhaps it was better thus.

Where would she go? What would she do? How would she fill her days? How long would the divorce take? Would Luke marry Caprice immediately? Could she look forward to a future when she would occasionally meet Caprice in London or at the houses of mutual friends and know that she was married to the man who had once been her husband? Or would Luke find it impossible to stay in England knowing such an embarrassing meeting could arise? Would he expect her to live abroad?

These and like questions caused her brain to spin. She stood at the window long after dawn streaked the sky with pink and gold and she rang for some tea just after seven.

Sitting in a deep armchair by her dressing-table, a cup of the hot, fragrant liquid at her side, Margo realised that it was now tomorrow—and she would have to face Luke and Caprice. All her logical arguments had suddenly deserted her and she could not think of a single reason why she should give up her husband to a woman who had always schemed to own him one day.

Her eyes ached with weariness and she was tired of thoughts. The night had been spent in a whirl of thoughts which left her brain numb and weary. She turned to gaze at her own reflection in the mirrors of her dressing-table—and she saw a pale-faced woman with deep violet shadows beneath her eyes and lines of tension about her mouth. Her long blonde hair flowed over her shoulders in a silken cascade and she thought how ridiculous it was that a woman of forty-four should have the hair of a girl. In the dim light of morning the silver strands were difficult to detect and her hair shone like a mass of spun gold.

She could not sit there all day with her hair down and the traces of last night's make-up haunting her skin. She rang the bell sharply and ordered her maid to run her bath and then lay out the hyacinth blue dress and stole.

When she was ready, she looked at herself again in the long mirror which was affixed to one of her bedroom walls.

She saw a slender, tall woman in a well-cut blue dress which enhanced the attractive lines of her figure. The stole was lightly draped about her shoulders. Her golden hair—and now the silver threads were visible—was swept up into a neat chignon at the back of her head, baring her proud forehead and emphasising the classic loveliness of her profile. She was carefully made up in order to hide the dark shadows beneath her blue eyes and the lines of pain about her mouth. Slim legs encased in silk stockings and high-heeled shoes of the same blue as her outfit completed the picture.

Margo smiled ironically. There was little point in seeking to look one's best for such an occasion—giving up one's husband to another woman! Did she hope to emphasise to Luke that his wife was still slim and lovely, despite twenty years of marriage and motherhood. Complete folly! Caprice possessed a rich and glowing beauty which she could never hope to outshine. There was an air of youth and vitality about Caprice which would linger when she was an old, old woman. Despite all her efforts, Margo did not look anything but what she was—a well-dressed and well-groomed wife and mother in her early forties. Caprice had that remarkable gift of looking never any older than twenty-five and she moved with the lithe grace of a young girl. All her movements and gestures were graceful. She glowed with vitality.

Margo addressed her own reflection lightly.

"Well, my dear, you've had a good innings—now you must retire gracefully and admit your defeat. If Luke had not been such a splendid person, Caprice would have won this battle many years ago."

She spun on her heel and left her room.

Luke was down to breakfast. There was no sign of Caprice or any of the young people. Margo halted on the threshold of the dining-room, a little taken aback. She had banked on having the meal alone or with the company of the children.

Certainly she did not want to breakfast with Luke and no other. But she came into the room and greeted him as she had greeted him every morning for twenty years.

"Good morning, Luke." She stooped to kiss his cheek.

He patted her hand, albeit a little awkwardly. "Good morning, my dear. You're looking very attractive this morning." The last words were spoken with a trace of surprise as though he had looked at his wife as a woman for the first time in many long months.

She slipped into her seat at the end of the table. "Where is everyone? Surely one night of festivities doesn't put them to bed for the day?"

Luke smiled and rose to help himself to fresh coffee. "Quite the reverse. Adam and Serena have gone out to exercise the horses. Francesca is having breakfast in bed but I think she is entitled to that as she certainly threw herself into all the festivities with zest and vigour."

"And . . . Caprice?" She was annoyed with herself for that momentary hesitation.

He continued to spoon sugar into his

coffee and merely said, without looking up: "Oh, she's following Francesca's example, I imagine. I haven't seen her this morning."

She nibbled a slice of toast. She felt that food was impossible to stomach while the ordeal lay ahead of her. She sipped at the coffee and managed to exchange a few exceedingly trivial remarks with her husband about the weather, about the children and about the previous night's ball.

Luke felt uncomfortable. He did not know whether Margo meant to carry on as though she had not overheard those enlightening words on the terrace—as he realised now, she had always carried on at times when many another woman would have screamed abuse and accusations at him, their minds riddled with suspicious jealousy and fear. Or was Margo merely biding her time before she exploded? Would she demand that Caprice leave the Hall never to be welcomed there again? He could not imagine this from Margo somehow—she was too cool and reasonable and far from vindictive. He could not remember one spiteful word against anyone during their married life. She had never said anything unkind about Caprice and in fact seemed to be fond of her— where he would expect resentment and hatred and spiteful venom she had always shown acceptance and affection and serenity.

At last he asked abruptly: "Do you still want to talk to me, Margo?"

She met his eyes calmly. "Yes, please, Luke. Have you any engagements this morning?"

He shook his head. "None at all."

"Then I'll come to the library when I've seen Cook," she said quietly. "We are less likely to be disturbed there."

He rose and crumpled his serviette. "Do you want to speak to me alone? Or—do you want Caprice to be present?"

She raised her head and looked at him for a long moment. Then she said: "What I have to say is for your ears alone, Luke."

He nodded. "Very well." He picked up the morning papers. "Do you want any of these?" he asked diffidently.

"No, thank you, Luke." She watched him walk from the room and despite her calm assurance she was filled with sympathy for his embarrassment.

13

LUKE leapt to his feet as the library door opened and Margo entered the room. It was partly from a natural courtesy—partly from the torment of his thoughts. He had tried to remember all that Margo must have overheard. Serena's youthful voice still rang in his ears—but what was more important was his own conversation with Caprice but this he could not remember with full accuracy. He remembered asking Caprice if he should take the childrens' advice and ask Margo for a divorce. He remembered too that he had assured Caprice that he wished to marry her. But now there was no longer time to extract the reluctant recollections from his brain for Margo entered looking neat and immaculate and strangely attractive. How unruffled her expression, how slow and strangely dignified her movements with the inner grace that was typical of her.

He pulled up a chair. "Will you sit

down?" he asked politely and then he felt like laughing at the ridiculous situation. This was his wife and he was treating her like an unexpected guest who was particularly unwelcome.

Margo sat down and asked him to give her a cigarette. Obediently he leaned forward and picked up the filigree box from the low table at his side. It was a very rare thing for Margo to smoke and he felt a little at ease as he recognised this as a sign of inward agitation. He flicked a lighter into life and she bent her head over the flame. She allowed the blue-grey smoke to filter into the air and watched its progress until it vanished into nothingness. Her life with Luke was similar to that intangible smoke—uncertain, vacillating and finally—nothing, she thought.

Their eyes met across the space which separated them. Then Margo said with the merest hesitation: "I'm prepared to give you your freedom, Luke."

He started with surprise. "But—Margo —do you realise what you're saying?"

She smiled briefly. "I haven't come in here to talk nonsense, my dear. Accidentally I overheard Serena and Adam talking last night. I know that you heard them too. Then I watched you and Caprice walk to the other end of the terrace and I deliberately followed you and listened to your conversation—a despicable thing to do, I know, but it certainly cleared up a few things which I've often wanted to know. Adam, for instance? I've never believed you unfaithful to me since we were married, Luke—but Adam was born before I married you. I've known for a long time now that you're in love with Caprice. I was very relieved to hear that Adam isn't your son and that nothing could prevent Serena from marrying him."

He was stunned for a brief moment. Then he said: "You've really thought Adam was mine?"

She shrugged briefly. "Only now and again—a vague suspicion."

He scanned her expression. "What other points were you dubious about, Margo?"

"Whether you would marry Caprice if you were both free? Sometimes a man wants most the thing that is out of his reach—and when he has the chance of taking it into his possession, he finds that all desire to own it has gone."

He pursed his lips. "That's sometimes true," he admitted. "But not with me. Are you serious, Margo? Are you really offering me my freedom so I can marry Caprice?"

"Yes, I am."

"But why? I mean—it's too generous of you . . ."

"And therefore suspicious," she finished for him. A brief smile played about her lips. "Are you wondering if I've something up my sleeve—another man perhaps? No, Luke. It's just that I've known for a long time how you felt about Caprice. It's obvious that she feels the same way about you. Have you ever found me to be unduly possessive? Vindictive?" Luke shook his head dumbly. "I know it's useless to hold on to a man when he wants to be free," she said coolly. "We'll never find the old peaceful contentment again, Luke. Even if you refused my offer, always there would be the memory of what I overheard last night between us." She sighed a little. "The children are aware of the circumstances—but they're growing up and beginning to notice things. They have modern ideas—you heard Serena and

Adam! Divorce will not shock or dismay them. It will be accepted without question."

Luke rose and began to pace the library, his hands thrust deep into trouser pockets. "Margo—Margo—you have everything cut and dried. You must have spent the whole night thinking this out. Are you sure about this? We've been married twenty years. We have three children. We have a great many friends who will be shocked and dismayed if our marriage breaks up. It will be difficult for both of us to start new lives." It was surprising how hurt he was to find her not only willing but actually eager to break the bonds which had tied them for so many years. It seemed suddenly too big a step. In his mind he reiterated that they had been married twenty years, that they had always been happy, that they were well used to one another, that she had always been a good wife to him, that they must consider the children . . . Not once did his thoughts turn to the anticipation of his freedom, the opportunity to love Caprice openly and to offer her an honourable proposal of marriage.

She was perfectly serene. "I have spent the night thinking everything out. I've quite made up my mind, Luke. It will be better in every way. Of course, it will be rather strange and difficult at first—" She smiled at him. "We're so used to one another, my dear. But habits—even of twenty years' standing—can be broken. The children will soon be reconciled to the way things are. Our friends will be distressed but they're intelligent enough to appreciate that sometimes it is impossible for two people to continue in a marriage that has become an intolerable burden."

Luke spun round and stared at her. All colour drained from his face and his heart beat with a slow thickness which made him feel veritably ill. "An intolerable burden," he repeated. "That is what our marriage is to you, Margo?" He spoke stiffly, with difficulty.

She rose and went to him, holding out her hands. "My dear, don't misunderstand me. I'm not implying that I've ever been unhappy or discontented. But nevertheless it is a burden to know that you would much rather live out the rest of your life with Caprice—and I don't like to think of myself as standing in your way."

"Luke has never allowed you to stand in his way," Caprice said quietly. Neither had heard the library door open or noticed her entry. Now she stood by the door, a rigid little figure, her eyes dark and burning in a pale face. "My dear Margo, if Luke ever really wanted to be with me, he would have left you years ago and carried me off from under Cliff's nose." She came further into the room.

Margo took a step towards her. "Caprice—this is a private conversation."

Caprice smiled slowly, mockingly. "But it very much concerns me. I've no right to listen to something not meant for my ears —but you're offering Luke his freedom. If he accepts he will automatically ask me to marry him—and I shall probably accept. So this private conversation of yours reacts very much on me and my wishes and feelings."

Luke moved forward quickly and took Caprice by the arm. "What did you mean, Caprice?" he asked urgently, his senses sharpened by the emotion of the scene and realising that her words had held a deeper import than Margo had sought.

Caprice shook off his hand. Lithely, gracefully, she sat down in the armchair that he had recently vacated and smiled up at both of them. "I am frequently amazed to find that so many otherwise charming and likeable people are complete and utter fools when it comes to love," she said slowly, assuredly. "Luke—listen to me. I've loved you for years—and I don't mind that Margo hears what I have to say. Twenty years ago, I would have married you without a second thought. Ten years ago I would still have married you if you had insisted that was our destiny. Now—though I've no doubt at all that Margo is being very self-sacrificing and offering to give you your freedom—now I wouldn't marry you if you went down on bended knee to me."

"Caprice!" The exclamation shot from his lips.

"It's true," she said. "We're too old, Luke. It's so silly to think of passionate love and daring all to get our heart's desire at our ages. I've no wish to see your perfectly admirable marriage dragged through the divorce courts for my sake. Luke, you wouldn't be happy with me, you know. Margo is the sort of woman you need as a wife—not a tempestuous, volatile person like me—and I'm still tempestuous even at forty-five. You're getting too old to cope with me and my tantrums and my whims. It's been very pleasant to nurse a secret love in your heart all these years and promise yourself that one day we'll be together. You're a romantic soul, my dear. But I think I've always known that the chance would come too late—and I don't regret it. All the arguments I've ever put up to you remain as strong as ever." She rose to her feet and went up to Luke. She took his face between her hands and kissed his lips fleetingly. "Count your blessings," she murmured. "And let us always remain the good friends we've been all these years." She smiled deep into his eyes and then she turned and took Margo's hands in hers. "Thank you," she said softly. "I do appreciate your motives—but don't be a fool. You love Luke—so do I but you have first claim. Hang on to him, my dear Margo—he'll never find similar happiness with anyone else as you've given him in twenty years of marriage."

She walked to the door and looked back with her eyes filled with laughter and a mocking smile just curving her lips.

Luke and Margo were hardly aware of her movement. For their eyes met across the room and Caprice knew that, difficult though it had been to deny the cry of her heart, she had done the right thing. There was the look about Luke of a man reprieved from the gallows. And in Margo's blue eyes was a dawning hope which threatened to destroy the cool composure of her expression.

"Now you can continue your private conversation," Caprice said lightly. "I've had my say—I hope you'll both come to your senses." And the library door closed firmly behind her.

Luke scanned Margo's face. "Well?" he murmured.

"I shall never understand Caprice," she returned. "I felt certain that she'd snatch you from me with barely a word of thanks." She laughed a little, a tinkle of a laugh, high-pitched and nervous.

"Will you think I'm a fool if I tell you

that far from feeling disappointed that Caprice doesn't want to marry me—I'm relieved?"

She came close to him and put her arms about him. It was the first impetuous and impulsive embrace he had known from her in many years. She smiled up into his face and her eyes were warm and tender and radiant. "I'd made up my mind to let you go, darling—but you know it would have broken my heart."

He caught her close and pressed his lips against her cheek. "What a strange woman you are, Margo!" he sighed. "You act as though I'm a stranger who's lived in the house for twenty years and you'll be glad to get rid of me—then you talk of a broken heart when the danger of losing me is over."

"I never could show my feelings very well," she reminded him. "I think Caprice knows me better than most people."

"She said that you loved me," he said gently.

"So I do. I've always loved you, Luke—now don't tell me that you've ever thought otherwise!"

He could not meet her eyes. Shamefacedly, he murmured against her golden hair: "To tell the truth, I've never thought about it very much. I suppose I've taken you for granted—I've always assumed that you love me without ever wondering how deep it went or whether it was still in existence." Now he sought her eyes and went on frankly: "As Caprice said, I've been nursing a secret love all these years and wanting something unattainable when something much more valuable has been close at hand. I've not given you a very fair deal, Margo."

"Nonsense!" she said firmly. "Have I ever made any complaints?"

"You've been wonderful," he assured her quickly.

She smiled at that, a slow, faintly embarrassed smile. "I've been very happy," she said sincerely. "Oh, moments when I've been depressed because of Caprice—times when I've wanted more from you than you've given me—but they haven't lasted long. I think I've always known that Caprice wasn't a very great menace—that if it was a question of choosing between us, I would win in the long run. And I learned very quickly that it's fatal to expect too much from anyone —now I only expect from you what you're prepared to give or are capable of giving and I've learnt where to find my happiness, Luke." She kissed his cheek warmly. "So I assure you, darling, that I've never had any regrets."

Swiftly and sincerely, he replied: "I've never had any regrets either, Margo. If I had, surely you know that I've had said to hell with everything long ago and persuaded Caprice to run off with me. Deep in my heart, I think I've always known that you offer a more lasting happiness and that quiet contentment is far better than wild ecstasy which would probably burn itself out quickly. Now I thank God that Caprice has always refused all my suggestions, that she has been sensible and wise for us both—for if I hurt you, my dear, I'd hurt myself. I suppose I've always loved you the most, Margo— but it's hard to realise it until one is faced with losing the one person who really matters. Now I know that my life would be nothing without you, Margo."

She sighed gently. "Do you know that

I've waited twenty years to have you say that to me, Luke?"

He caught her to him and kissed her mouth with sweet tenderness and the merest hint of passion. It was joy to Margo to know her husband's arm about her and his lips on hers for she had been convinced that never again would she know his nearness and his affectionate caresses. She still found it hard to believe that she would not have to sacrifice her own happiness for his sake: that he and Caprice did not want to be together in the future that lay ahead; that she could carry on as Luke's wife and still know the contentment and happiness that she had always known with him.

He held her a little way from him and searched her eyes anxiously. "Margo, you will believe me if I swear to you that I've never been unfaithful to you—with Caprice or anyone else?"

She felt like crying out that it did not matter if Caprice had been his mistress: that she had never been made to suffer because of it, if it were so; that she had always known so much more than passion from her beloved husband—far more important things, such as kindness, affec-

tionate consideration, shared pain and
sorrow and anxiety, years of companionship and friendship.

But she merely said quietly, serenely: "I
know that, Luke. You aren't capable of
treachery. I would have known years ago
if you'd betrayed me with another woman
—and you would have had your freedom
then, when you wanted it, not when I
offered it too late."

He amended her words, first kissing her
mouth lightly: "Not too late—when I no
longer want it. I'm trying to impress on
you that I never actively wanted to be free,
anyway. Do you really believe that I'd
have let you, the children, or anything else
stand in my way if I'd really thought the
world well lost for love? You see, Caprice
knows me better than I know myself—
she's always said so. She knew that deep
down you were the one who mattered, the
only one capable of making me happy for
all time and not just a few months or
years."

"You've always had a strong sense of
duty, Luke," Margo pointed out.

"Duty? What man cares about duty
when he's caught in the throes of love and

passion?" he demanded. "If it's real love and lasting passion. I successfully deluded myself that Caprice was the woman I loved with every fibre of my being. Be honest, Margo—do you think I could have married you and been happy if I really loved another woman with such intensity?"

In her heart, Margo knew with certainty that Luke had loved Caprice: did in fact still love her. But he was a moral coward and could not face the break-up of a twenty-year old marriage at his time of life. Perhaps he knew that Caprice would be a demanding and passionate wife; he was getting to the age when passion was no longer of first importance, and content-ment and peace were more likely to appeal to his senses than rapture and tumult. She admired Caprice still more for voluntarily surrendering to the fact that Luke's wife had first claim. It could not have been easy for her to give Luke up after all these years and now that happiness seemed within her embrace. If Caprice loved Luke with only a third of the love within her being that burned in Margo's heart, then it had been indeed difficult—so Margo felt a surge of affectionate admiration and respect. It was better that Luke should stay with her now. She could make him happier in the later years of his life than Caprice: no man wanted to make a new life at fifty—and no one could deny that Luke was very near to fifty these days. Still handsome, distinguished, and active—but almost fifty nonetheless.

So she smiled tremulously and assured him: "No, I don't think you could have, Luke," knowing full well that he had done that very thing. "But you would never have listened if I'd tried to tell you that," she added gently. "It was something you had to discover for yourself."

"Now I know—and I'll never behave like a love-struck adolescent again. Forgive me, Margo—for not realising years ago how much I love you."

She kissed him with real ardency and emotion. She believed that he had woken to a new realisation how much she meant to him. But nothing would induce her to believe that he placed her before Caprice in his heart—and she was content that it should be thus. One could find a great deal of happiness even in coming second in a man's life.

She met his eyes frankly. "The look on your face when I told you that I'd give you your freedom absolved you from any reason for my forgiveness, Luke. You looked like a man who'd received his death sentence—and I knew beyond any doubt that you value our marriage above everything else." That was true enough, she felt. He valued it because it represented a reliable foundation for living: a mark of a man's success in something he had determined to do well; a steady solidity of home, wife and family, an indication that another Fortune had done his duty well in these matters.

"It's the best thing that ever happened in my life," he said warmly, confirming her thoughts. "It's made up for a great many things, Margo. We've been so very fortunate, my dear. Twenty years with hardly a cross word, very few heartaches, and not many sorrows to beset us. Three attractive children who've always been both healthy and intelligent—who are now growing up into pleasant and responsible adults. And there are still many years ahead of us, Margo—so much more happiness waiting for us."

"But you still regret that you didn't get Veerham," she said quietly. "You regret that you and Cliff were not as close as you should have been: and you would have liked Adam to be your son."

He was startled by her insight. For a long moment he considered her words. Then he said slowly: "Both Adam and Serena are very young but I believe that one day they will be married. I'll raise no objection and so I shall be able to call Adam 'son'. Veerham will in time belong to their son—God willing!—our grandchild, Margo—and that will erase the last seed of regret that Veerham didn't come to me. As for Cliff, we were worlds apart as children. We never cared much for each other but that didn't stop me grieving for him when he died and wishing that we could have been friends while he lived. But that's in the past—and it's the present and future that seems to demand all my attention now, my dear."

"And Caprice?" She could not resist the question.

He frowned a little. "Oh, she'll go on

enjoying life in her inimitable way until she's about ninety. We needn't worry about Caprice. She's perfectly satisfied with her life as it is—and I know she spoke the truth when she said that she wouldn't marry me were I free. Caprice likes her freedom, you know. She's an independent person—and I doubt if anyone—even me," and he said this without conceit, "could mean as much to her as Adam does."

In which he was wrong, for Caprice had denied her very heart-beats when she relinquished all claim to Luke, realising how matters stood when she saw his stricken face and felt sure what Margo had said to him. Now, more than ever, it seemed that their love was futile—she would not believe that he had ceased to love her for they had shared a rare emotion that comes to few men and women. But she could understand that opportunity had come too late—with every passing year the need to be with each other all the time had faded a little. Desire was no longer so swift to rise: the blood moved slower in their veins; the years were making themselves felt in various ways and Caprice was convinced that snatching at happiness like two children would not make for a lasting peace of mind.

Now, they could never know regret for they had never hurt anyone by their love for each other. But if they had allowed Margo to free Luke so that they could marry, behind their happiness would always be the lurking guilt that they had taken Margo's rights away from her.

So Caprice was sad and yet resigned to the path which destiny had chosen for her footsteps.

14

HE was a tall man and he cast a long shadow as he stood by the lake with the sun high overhead. He stared across the water and he looked beyond its cool dark depths, the trees which fringed it on the other side throwing their own tall shadows across the water's edge; he looked at a house which was set high in a clearing and even from this distance he could pick out the blaze of colour which was the flower gardens.

He stood and looked at the house and his thoughts winged back to the time when he had stood in this very same spot twenty five years ago and wondered how he would ever live without Veerham as his own, bitterly resentful that his father had allotted Fortune Hall to him and Veerham to Cliff.

Twenty-five years. It was a long time and Cliff had been dead for twelve of them. His son Adam was Lord Veerham and that morning he had married Luke's daughter, Serena. The service had taken place in the small and ancient church of St. Peter's in Mallingham. Weddings were no longer the very fashionable and crowded affairs they had been and only a small group of guests stood in the quiet coolness of the old church to witness the ceremony.

His beloved Serena. How beautiful she had been in her short dress of white nylon lace, the small Juliet cap with the short veil adorning her red-gold crop of curls. How radiant her lovely face as she looked up at Adam—how eagerly their hands had met and remained linked while the same vicar—much older now—who had married her parents and christened her, performed the marriage rites.

He gladly welcomed Adam as a son. He had always loved and admired the boy who had grown into such a handsome and integral young man. He felt no hestitation at all in giving Serena into Adam's care. He knew that they had loved each other since childhood and that marriage had always been their one aim. During the last five years, they had drifted apart a little. Serena had been more than difficult, insisting on a career rather than marriage, confusing poor Adam with promises of an early wedding one moment and then denying that she would ever marry the next. But he had been faithful and patient —and now at last they were married. He wondered if Serena had been a little afraid of marriage. She was still young—only twenty one now—and this had been one of the excuses she frequently offered on the altar of procrastination. But through it all ran the thread of her love for Adam— and everyone had been confident that she would eventually marry him—but in her own good time.

His eyes were tender as he surveyed the estate which had come to mean so much to him and knew that the yearning for Veerham no longer had the power to awaken despair in his heart. It seemed that throughout his life he had been compelled to accept second best and eventually that second best proved itself to be more valuable than the first choice.

He turned away from the lake and he fumbled in the pocket of his old and shabby tweed jacket for his faithful friend —his pipe. He thrust it between his teeth and clamped down on it hard as he turned his footsteps back the way he had walked. He had changed from formal clothes as soon as Adam and Serena had left the Hall in Adam's bright red sports car on their way to Italy for their honeymoon. Without a word to the guests who lingered on at the Hall to discuss the wedding and enjoy further glasses of champagne, he had slipped away for a few moments of quiet solitude and thought.

A lump rose suddenly in his throat for he thought of Margo and the ache for her presence was intolerable in that moment. His life seemed empty and lonely without her. She had been a wonderful wife to him. It was poignantly true that he had never realised how much she did to make his life comfortable and happy until she left him. A year ago now she had slipped away to another world in her sleep.

He had not even known about the malignant disease which gradually possessed her until death came to relieve her from pain —a merciful and blessed release which helped Luke to forgive himself for his ignorance. She had never been a complaining wife. She kept her pain to herself, hugging it and befriending it without a word of reproach against cruel destiny which had brought her to such a pass. Luke felt that she had been wrong to keep him in ignorance—but remembering how she had always tried to spare him from anxiety or unhappiness, he could understand her motive.

He wished that she could have been with him on this glorious summer day and seen their youngest daughter married to Adam. She had always encouraged the match and Luke felt that her one regret when she knew she was dying was that still Serena had not fixed the wedding day.

It seemed so wrong to him that Margo should never have known the joy of seeing her children happily and safely married, of holding grandchildren in her arms and watching them at play, of looking forward to an old age with her husband.

Until her death, he had not realised how very much he owed to Margo. But then —as now—he had been immeasurably grateful that he had not seized the chance to find happiness with Caprice. At least he had the comfort of knowing that the last few years had been happy ones for Margo

—and he had never regretted his cowardice. For it had been nothing but fear of the unknown which prevented him from taking his freedom and marrying Caprice. He had been married to Margo for twenty years. They had gone through the good and bad years together. They had known a great deal of happiness and they were used to each other. Nearing fifty, it had suddenly struck him forcibly that to start a new kind of life then was full of risks and did not guarantee happiness. He might be leaping out of the frying-pan into the fire—but he did not put it as easily as that even in his thoughts. Caprice had seemed quite ready to forfeit any happiness with him. In fact she had said plainly that they were too old for romance. Later, this had worried him because only the previous evening she had assured him that they were never too old while they loved each other. Perhaps she had never really loved him.

But he dismissed this instantly. Caprice had loved him completely as he had loved her—but she had realised fully what it would entail for him to break with Margo after twenty years and marry her—and no doubt she sensed the fear and doubts in him. Doubts that he had no right to feel because his love for Caprice had always been a very real thing.

As he strode around the lakeside, he mused on the dangers and difficulties which beset a confused and bewildered human being on the road of life. At every turn in the road, one came to a decision—which path to take now? Two paths led in different directions and their destination was out of sight. One had to choose between the two paths never knowing which would turn out to be the right one. The decision could only be made by oneself and it was a hard decision to make. Sometimes it was best to make a snap decision on impulse without thinking too much about the consequences. Other times it was better to think it over very carefully and occasionally decide on taking the path which was against one's own will and yet could lead to happiness or safety for someone else. It was very surprising how often things turned out for the best—a platitude which had always annoyed him and yet invariably was proved right.

He could not have known that Margo

would die within a few years of that important decision. So he had been influenced only by his own fear of a new step in life and a feeling of duty to his wife after twenty years of loyalty on her side. If he had insisted on his freedom and married Caprice, he would never have forgiven himself for allowing Margo to live alone and unhappy for the last few years of her life.

He approached the path which led through the woods to the house and then it was that he heard a faint rustle of skirts, the sharp crack of a twig underfoot. He felt a prickling of hair on the back of his neck and suddenly his mouth was dry. The tension of his nerves and the sudden racing of his heart told him that the woman he loved had come in search of him and his pace quickened instinctively.

She rounded a corner and paused briefly at sight of him. Then her eyes lit up with a warm glow and her lips curved into a slow, rich smile. She moved forward quickly and with the lithe grace of that natural movement the years fell from her and he remembered those few wonderful days she had shared with him at the Hall many years ago.

She had been at the wedding of course. She had been staying at the Hall for the last week—but now it seemed that he set eyes on her for the first time in many long and weary months. She had been formally charming to him, treating him very much as the father of the girl her son was going to marry. He had respected her response to conventionality. But now she moved towards him and he thought of her only as Caprice, the woman he loved and had always loved. Happiness seemed suddenly close at hand.

She put out her hands and his own closed over them involuntarily. "Dear Luke," she murmured. "I felt sure I'd find you here."

He smiled down at her. "I'm getting old, Caprice. I need visual aid to memory. I've been wandering around down here, going back over the long years. It seems hard to believe that my Serena is now a grown up and very self-possessed young woman—a married woman—when I can remember her vividly playing in the waters and around the edges of the lake."

Her eyes were warmly ardent. "Can you remember a time when you wandered hand in hand with me—and didn't know that I loved you, Luke? Or is that a memory best forgotten?"

His hands tightened on hers convulsively. "I remember many things about you, Caprice. I've only had memories to sustain me for many years, my dear."

She scanned his face: it was older now and yet still handsome in the vital Fortune claim to good looks. His eyes were inexpressibly weary as though he had sought all his life for something that refused to be found. There was a hint of loneliness about his mouth and his eager clasp of her hands betrayed that in his heart still lived a vibrant love for her.

They turned and walked onwards to the house. Now she had linked her hand in his arm. "I wish Margo could have been here to see our radiant young people married," Caprice said with a brief sigh.

Luke nodded. "She was confident of the outcome, my dear," he said musingly. "While everyone else despaired of ever seeing them married, Margo knew that it would happen one day. I often think that she had a remarkable gift of insight into the future, you know."

Caprice looked straight ahead. Her voice was husky and musical still but it trembled a little as she asked: "And what do you think she saw in your future, Luke—when she knew that soon she would die and leave you alone?"

He shrugged. "I haven't a future any more, Caprice. I'm fifty-three now—all I'm concerned with is doing my best to live the present. I can only look forward to old age and, possibly, grandchildren."

"What a dismal thought!" Caprice exclaimed. She looked up at Luke and squeezed his arm. Her eyes were bright now with laughter. Looking down into those dark, glowing eyes, he was struck anew by the rich vitality of her personality which had never faded one iota for all the many years which snatched so much from the average human being. "One never knows what lies ahead," she went on. "I'll never admit to being old—because then one admits that life holds nothing more. Which will never be true for me! I'm fifty-one. Now that I've washed my hands of Adam, convinced that he's chosen the best

290

possible girl as his wife, I intend to start living my own life again."

Luke could not repress a smile. It began in a brief quirk of the lips—then at last it spread into a full rich smile and a gurgle of amusement broke from him. "What a wonderful woman you are!" he exclaimed. "Oh, Caprice—how I envy you!"

She stopped and faced him squarely. "But I don't want to go on living alone, Luke. I've had enough of it. I'm not cut out for a solitary existence. All my life I've wanted to be loved and desired and needed. I made a mistake with Cliff—I paid for it time and time again. I've done my duty by Adam—a much-loved duty, I'll add, and I've never grudged him a moment of my time or attention. Now I want to think only of myself—and my happiness . . ." She broke off and her eyes appealed to him. "Oh, Luke—you don't make things any easier for me, do you?" Her tone was half-laughing, half-reproachful.

He searched her face and found what he sought. A sigh escaped him—a thankful sigh. Then he drew her slowly into his arms and kissed her with eager love and passion—as he had not kissed any woman since the last time he held Caprice in his arms. Then he raised his head and said quietly: "I've asked you many times to be my mistress—to let us both know a little happiness. But I've never been able to ask you to be my wife—but you know that's what I've always wanted, my darling. We've both waited for so many years. Will you marry me, Caprice?"

There was no hesitation. "Yes, of course. I was afraid I'd have to ask you to marry me—I would have done too. I've wanted you so long—now perhaps we'll be able to find our happiness together, darling." She cupped his face in her two slender hands and raised herself on her toes. She pressed her lips tenderly against his mouth. A fleeting kiss yet it spoke volumes. "Dear Luke," she murmured gently and as ever her words were an endearment which sped swiftly to his heart.

GUIDE
TO THE COLOUR CODING
OF
ULVERSCROFT BOOKS

Many of our readers have written to us expressing their appreciation for the way in which our colour coding has assisted them in selecting the Ulverscroft books of their choice. To remind everyone of our colour coding—this is as follows:

BLACK COVERS
Mysteries

★

BLUE COVERS
Romances

★

RED COVERS
Adventure Suspense and General Fiction

★

ORANGE COVERS
Westerns

★

GREEN COVERS
Non-Fiction

ROMANCE TITLES
in the
Ulverscroft Large Print Series

THE SHADOWS
OF THE CROWN TITLES
in the
Ulverscroft Large Print Series

The Tudor Rose   *Margaret Campbell Barnes*
Brief Gaudy Hour *Margaret Campbell Barnes*
Mistress Jane Seymour   *Frances B. Clark*
My Lady of Cleves

Margaret Campbell Barnes
Katheryn The Wanton Queen

Maureen Peters
The Sixth Wife   *Jean Plaidy*
The Last Tudor King   *Hester Chapman*
Young Bess   *Margaret Irwin*
Lady Jane Grey   *Hester Chapman*
Elizabeth, Captive Princess   *Margaret Irwin*
Elizabeth and The Prince of Spain

Margaret Irwin
Gay Lord Robert   *Jean Plaidy*
Here Was A Man   *Norah Lofts*
Mary Queen of Scotland:
The Triumphant Year   *Jean Plaidy*
The Captive Queen of Scots   *Jean Plaidy*
The Murder in the Tower   *Jean Plaidy*
The Young and Lonely King   *Jane Lane*
King's Adversary   *Monica Beardsworth*
A Call of Trumpets   *Jane Lane*